LORD OF THE
MOUNTAIN

RONALD KIDD

Albert Whitman & Company
Chicago, Illinois

Other books by Ronald Kidd

Room of Shadows
Night on Fire
Dreambender

Library of Congress Cataloging-in-Publication
data is on file with the publisher.

Text copyright © 2018 by Ronald Kidd
Cover art copyright © 2018 by Albert Whitman & Company
Cover art by Carolyn Arcabascio
First published in the United States of America
in 2018 by Albert Whitman & Company
ISBN 978-0-8075-4751-9
"Bury Me Under the Weeping Willow," "Lonesome Valley," "The Wandering
Boy," "Wildwood Flower," "Don't Forget This Song," "Room in Heaven for Me,"
"Sunshine in the Shadows," and "When the World's on Fire" by A.P. Carter
Used by Permission of Peer International Corporation. All Rights Reserved.
"Lord of the Mountain" lyric by Ronald Kidd. Used by permission
of Ronald Kidd. All rights reserved.

Disclaimer: This is a work of fiction. All of the characters, organizations,
and events portrayed in this novel are either products of the author's
imagination or are used fictitiously. This book is not endorsed by
or affiliated with or sponsored by the Carter family.

Printed in the United States of America
10 9 8 7 6 5 4 3 2 1 BP 22 21 20 19 18

For more information about Albert Whitman & Company,
visit our website at www.albertwhitman.com.

To the memory of Paul and Ida Sue Kidd,
to my Southern family and friends, and,
as always, to Yvonne and Maggie

PROLOGUE

For a long time, I thought it was a dream.

A melody curled through the night, like a white ribbon on black. The tune was sad, but somehow I found it comforting. It was familiar, but I didn't know why. I followed it in my mind the way you'd follow a path, wondering where it led. Before I got there, I always woke up.

But the melody stayed. I hummed it in my head. I held it close. I hid it, like a secret. It had to be a secret, because Daddy hated music and would not allow it in his church or in our house. He said music was a sin, an abomination, a stain on God's robe.

Then one night, when Daddy was gone, I woke up and the melody didn't stop. There were words.

> Lord of the mountain
> Father on high
> Bend down and bless me
> Please won't you try

I tiptoed into the kitchen. Mama was making cornbread. As she baked, she sang. I gasped to hear music in our house. Mama whirled around, shock twisting her face. At the time, I thought the shock was about me, but now I think it was about her—how the melody had bubbled up inside without her thinking about it, then overflowed like water in a basin.

The song was real. It wasn't a dream. I had heard it, that night and the nights before when the song had floated by and found a place in my heart.

Now, watching the look of horror on Mama's face, I knew the song was important. It was dangerous. It had to be covered up and tamped down. I tried to ask about it, but she shushed me and told me never to speak of it again.

Mama's song was the key to everything, though I didn't know it then. It shaped my family. It lived in our house. It soothed us, then gripped us. I longed to know more about it, and that longing led me out the door, through the town, over the rails, and into the mountains.

PART I

WHEN THE WORLD'S ON FIRE

I'm going to heaven when the world's on fire
And I want God's bosom to be my pillow
Tide me over in the Rock of Ages
Rock of Ages cleft for me

—A. P. Carter, "When the World's on Fire"

CHAPTER 1

Mr. Fowler was barking again.

It was loud and frenzied, like you'd get if you teased a bulldog or yanked a Doberman's chain. Mr. Fowler was a large man, and when the spirit moved, he would dance and quiver and get circles of sweat under his arms. If the night was warm and the moon was just right, he would bark.

It wasn't so unusual, really. Mr. Bunn hopped. Mrs. Greeley chirped like a bird. Constance Carpenter, a girl not much older than me, babbled in a language no one had ever heard, except for those of us who showed up every Saturday night at the Church of Consecrated Heaven and Satan's on the Run.

Does that sound crazy to you? It did to me. The whole thing—the barking, the babbling, the hopping, the church itself, if you could call it that—had sprung, fully formed, from Daddy's head into the world. It was as if he had reached inside, grabbed the twisted part, and held it up, writhing and sputtering, for everyone to see. And the people had come.

Of course, they might never have known it was a church if it hadn't been for the sign, made by my father in a fit of holy painting. Put plainly, it was a tent.

Daddy had spotted the tent in a catalog, placed a phone call, and a few weeks later, a truck backed up to our house and unloaded a wooden crate bigger than my room.

Daddy paid the driver with what I later found out was the last of our savings. Then he got a crowbar and a couple of hammers, and the two of us set upon the crate. By the end of the day, using printed instructions and the occasional shouted tip from my little brother, Arnie, we had put up the tent in the empty lot next to our house.

That evening, as the sun set, Daddy called Mama, and the four of us stood at the entrance while he prayed. This wasn't one of your sentence prayers, or even paragraph or chapter. It was a volume prayer, one you could set right up next to A–Z in Collier's Encyclopedia. He prayed us up and down, back and forth, in and out. He started at the beginning, which for him was the typhoid fever that had descended like Moses's locusts one terrible day and carried my big sister, named Sister, off to heaven.

We had lived in North Carolina at the time, in a town called Deep Gap, but I didn't remember any of it since I was barely two years old. Even so, that day was fresh in my mind because Daddy talked about it all the time. He got stuck on that day, in life and in his prayers. Mama told me it nearly killed him. Until finally, one night in the pouring rain, he disappeared and she found him in the cemetery, hugging Sister's grave, trying to climb in.

It was clear that Daddy needed strong medicine, so Mama packed the two of us in the car and drove to Bristol, Tennessee, where a famous traveling preacher named Billy Sunday was saving souls. She found where he was preaching and marched up to the front, dragging Daddy with one hand and me with the other, and she asked for a healing. Billy Sunday prayed over Daddy, and for good measure, he kissed me on top of the head, or so I was told.

Maybe the healing worked. Maybe it was just a band-aid on a gaping wound. Whatever it was, Daddy decided he wanted to live after all. But he didn't want to do it in North Carolina because of all the memories and the pain. He and Mama liked Bristol, so they decided to move there. They found a little wooden house that had a fresh coat of white paint, never mind the crooked floors and leaky roof. It had a kitchen for Mama and bedrooms for them and for me, though I had to share mine with Arnie when he came along a couple of years later.

We started going to a little church down the block, and sometimes during the service Daddy would sweat and mumble, talking to Sister like she was sitting there beside us. The church closed a few years later, but Daddy kept reading the Bible by himself. He would look up, wild-eyed, quoting scripture at us.

Mama would say, "That's fine, dear," but I can tell you it wasn't fine. It was dark and scary, and so was he, like maybe he'd been sucked into that grave after all. He had never been very religious, but now he took his Bible everyplace, and Jesus was his best friend.

Daddy worked at the lumber mill for a long time, and people there started calling him "the reverend." They would smile and shake their heads when they said it. In those days everybody went to church, but Daddy was something different, something strange. It made life hard sometimes. People would ask me about him, and I'd just chuckle or change the subject.

It wasn't easy being part of that family. We were an unusual group—odd to look at, odder still in what we did. Mama and Daddy were like the mismatched dishes we ate out of—his chipped and flawed, hers delicate and perfect, nearly weightless, so thin and fine that you could hold it up to the window and light would shine through.

Daddy was big, with ruddy skin, ears that stuck out, and an expression that made you either want to hug him or hit him. Mama was lovely, with white skin and long, black hair, but her rough hands showed that she wasn't afraid to work, and she did plenty of it when Daddy was off in the clouds. I don't know how they met, and they didn't like to talk about it. I do know they were devoted to each other in a way I never understood.

I got to be ten years old, then twelve and thirteen. Arnie made it to third grade, propelled by Mama's casseroles and a spirit that she said could be bottled and sold. He started off little and stayed little, with sandy-blond hair and freckles, and from the beginning, he followed Daddy around like a miniature shadow.

Then one day at the mill, God spoke to Daddy in a buzz saw. A few weeks later he quit his job, ordered the tent, and we had a new life.

Only it wasn't a tent. It was a church. Daddy made that clear from the beginning. A few days after it arrived, when the spirit grabbed him and stuck a paintbrush in his hand, we learned the name, which he said had come to him in a fever dream.

"Satan's on the run!" he told us at breakfast that morning.

"We know, dear," said Mama.

"No, I mean it's the name. That's what we'll call the church."

I must have rolled my eyes, because Mama kicked me under the table. Arnie, meanwhile, was hanging on every word. Within a few weeks he would be cooking up ways to help Daddy and even outdo him, eventually succeeding in a manner that scared the town half to death and nearly ruined everything.

"Wait!" said Daddy. He cocked his head, like he was picking up signals from outer space. "Poor, sweet Sister says she doesn't want to be left out. We also have to name the church after her home."

"Her home?" I asked.

Daddy looked at me like I was slow. "Consecrated heaven," he declared. "The Church of Consecrated Heaven and Satan's on the Run. That's what we'll call it."

He jumped up from breakfast and ran out to the garage, where he kept his paint. Next thing we knew, the church had a name. It was outlined in red to remind us (said Daddy) of Jesus's precious blood.

Soon he was praising the Lord, spouting scripture, and welcoming people into the tent, where they got his version of torture and salvation. Somehow they loved it—not all of them, but enough to fill the offering plates and pay him more than he'd ever made at the lumber mill.

I lived in Daddy's world, but not by choice. Like the tent in summer, it was a hot, stuffy place that threatened to smother you. It was a place where Jesus was king, but Daddy was in charge, a place where the train to heaven had jumped the rails. A place I desperately needed to escape.

CHAPTER 2

I'm Nathan Owens. My friends, the few that I made outside the tent flaps, called me Nate. The year was 1927. I was thirteen years old, and I was growing up in pieces. I had big feet, skinny arms, a puny little chest, and a good-sized Adam's apple. My nose was large, and I had squinty, little eyes, or so Arnie told me. He was eight and thought he was thirty.

People said I looked like Daddy, and I guess I did on the outside. The inside was another matter. Maybe inside I was like Mama. Or maybe I was like nobody, an impostor in the family, a stranger in my own body.

This is my story. I'm telling it to knit the parts of me together. I'm not sure where my story came from, but I know it's important, not just because it has the Carter Family in it. I'm in there too. Nate Owens. Living, breathing, breaking free, doing things because I want to, not because I'm told.

Daddy had a story, but it was different from mine. It started in life and flew up to include Jesus and *his* daddy, then down to my family and most especially to my sister, Sister, rest her soul, then even farther down to the devil, who Daddy had strong feelings about.

"His name is Satan," Daddy told Arnie and me. "A name is a sign of respect, and you need to respect Satan. Be on the lookout, boys."

Daddy's story, the one he built his church on, was a strange stew of Jesus and Satan, fishes and loaves, cornbread and Coca-Cola. It started with Bible verses and slithered through the vilest mayhem you could ever think about, like a slug through garbage. Sin was a big part of it. It's a part of us all, claimed Daddy. He said there was glory too, like when you turned from sin and came forward for baptism in Beaver Creek. Daddy would dunk you for all he was worth. There'd be a splash, and if the sun was just right, Daddy said you could look up at the clouds and see a dove. I'd seen a buzzard, a vulture, maybe a few pigeons, but never a dove.

Daddy's religion was a do-it-yourself affair. He took the parts that suited him and ignored the others, like he was shopping for clothes at J. C. Penney. Adam and Eve? Sure. Resurrection? Bring it on. Sin? Oh my, yes. Forgiveness? Not so fast. Free will? We'll get back to you on that. Science? The purest hogwash.

Music?

That was the strangest and most maddening of all. David had a harp. Gideon had a trumpet. The psalmist had songs. But Daddy's religion had no music.

Music, he told us, was Satan's tune. Don't think it. Don't

imagine it. And certainly don't do it. Every once in a while, old Mr. Beckham in the third row back would get wound up on Jesus and start whistling weird melodies, sounding halfway between a songbird and a teapot. Daddy would hurry over, grip Mr. Fowler's head like a grapefruit, and squeeze. That usually stopped him.

Daddy hated music. He refused to discuss it and couldn't abide hearing it. When I asked him why, he got a crazy look in his eye. He ranted and raved, and he turned bright red. Then he blinked and his face went slack.

The more he ranted about music, the more I was drawn irresistibly to it. His sermons, combined with Mama's song, pulled me to music like ants to honey. It was sweet. It was forbidden. It contained secrets that I could only imagine and did—endlessly.

One day in the kitchen, I asked Mama why Daddy hated music, and she shook her head. "You know we don't talk about that."

I must have been feeling either brave or stupid, because I said, "You sang. I heard you."

She shot me a look so hot that it burned, like the time I used sunlight and a magnifying glass to kill a bug. I stepped away, scorched, but I didn't forget.

Daddy and I were searching for something, but in different places. He looked in the tent, in the people who were drawn there by color and confusion and certainty. I didn't like it there. Sometimes, when the place was packed and the night was hot, I couldn't breathe. Mama noticed. She'd put her arm around my shoulders, and I'd be okay for a little while.

Mama was always there. She loved Daddy, even if sometimes she had to drag him to places for his own good. She figured that if he wanted to put up a tent and preach, so be it. She greeted people at the door and baked apple pie for fellowship hour. She tried to help Daddy, no matter how odd his plans might seem. His plans were her plans. That's what she told us. Jesus said you can build on rock or sand, and Mama was the rock. I guess I was sand.

We liked Bristol—a town like me. Bristol was divided, smack on the border between Tennessee and Virginia. The border ran down the middle of State Street, so when you crossed the street, you were passing from one state to another, the way I passed from Daddy's world to the real world and back again.

Sometime in the 1800s, an argument had started between the two halves of town. It seemed that the police from one side refused to chase a murderer across the border to the other side, and he got away. It made people bitter for a while, but then the two halves patched things up and had gotten along ever since.

When electric lights came to Bristol, a sign was erected over State Street that was made of metal and light bulbs. At first it said Push—That's Bristol, but no one knew what it meant. So they ran a contest for a new slogan and changed the sign.

Bristol
Va.   Tenn.
A Good Place to Live

Bristol was known for that sign and for other things too. One year, gasoline spilled into Beaver Creek, and the creek caught fire. I guess even water can burn. For some people, I suppose Bristol was also known for Daddy's preaching and for that big tent—flapping in the wind, yellow as an old bruise.

From the beginning, Daddy held services on Saturday night, not Sunday. He said Saturday was the Sabbath, and besides, that was the time he could go toe-to-toe with Satan. He would stand in the pulpit, which he had built out of a wheelbarrow and an orange crate, and tell the people why.

"Saturday night is Satan's time," Daddy bellowed, pointing his finger like a gun. "People drink, dance, play music. They curse and say, 'Go to hell.' I say yes, by God. Every Saturday night we'll go to hell and bring Jesus with us. He's stronger than whiskey and hotter than flames. Satan will feel the heat and take off running. He'll hop and skitter and jump, like he was dancing on coals. Meanwhile here's ol' Jesus, just glowing."

The world was having fun on Saturday night, but we were in Daddy's tent, battling the devil. Daddy loved it. Arnie loved it. Mama put up with it.

Me? I just wanted to get out of there.

CHAPTER 3

The stars were spread across the sky like Arnie's jacks on the living room floor, times a billion. Did God play games? Was he up there scattering the stars, then bouncing a ball and scooping them up? You win—here's a happy life. You lose—goodbye, Sister.

My science teacher, Mr. Wafford, said the stars are so far away that the light we see today is from millions of years ago. For all we know, the stars have exploded and we just don't realize it yet. We keep preaching and praying on Saturday night, talking to a God who could be destroying worlds as we speak. It's something to think about.

I was looking at the stars because, inside the tent, healing had broken out. In the middle of his sermon, Daddy had pulled little Jerry Witherspoon from the tenth row, and Jerry had limped forward. He had broken his leg on the school playground, and Daddy proposed to fix it, like Jesus did in the Bible.

Daddy asked the congregation to come forward and help, which meant laying their hands on Jerry. I knew for a fact that when people came forward, Lester Collins laid his hands on Bobbie Jo Bainbridge, and I seriously doubt that any healing happened.

I wasn't in a healing mood, so when the people crowded forward, I sneaked out the back. I made my way across the wet grass to a low stone wall behind the tent, sat down, and gazed at the stars.

It was a warm June night. The crickets were chirping. All around me, little yellow lights flickered on and off. They were lightning bugs. I noticed they flew in a zone, not too low and not too high. They knew what to do and where to do it. It was built into them. I wished I had a zone. I wanted to do things but didn't know what.

I thought about going to the graveyard, across the street from our house. It was an ancient place, called East Hill Cemetery. Generations of Bristol folks were buried there, including Joseph R. Anderson, who founded and named Bristol in 1852. One end of the cemetery was taken up by Confederate and Union soldiers who died in the Civil War.

I think the cemetery was one reason Daddy had picked our house. Death had brought us to Bristol that rainy night when Daddy had latched on to Sister's grave. And someday death, he figured, would take us away. It could happen in an instant, like a blessing, if you just keeled over. Or maybe, if you turned your back on God, you'd be swept away in a holy wind or consumed in a ball of fire. Either way, the cemetery would be right there, waiting.

Me, I found it peaceful. When I finished my chores, sometimes I'd head across the street and wander among the graves, touching the stones, tracing the names with my finger, trying to imagine who was buried there—a child the age of Sister, a soldier in uniform, someone like me.

There were voices from the tent. Daddy prayed, and the people clapped and called encouragement. Constance Carpenter babbled God knows what. There may have been a bark.

I heard music.

For a moment I thought it was coming from the tent, but of course that couldn't be. I listened more closely and realized the music came from beyond the wall. There were trees back there and a hill with a house on top. The house had been vacant when we had raised the tent, but recently some workers had come and started fixing up the place. They had finished, and a few weeks ago a family had moved in. Somebody said they were rich.

I swung around on the wall until I straddled it. On one side, people shouted and praised Jesus. On the other side, thin and wispy, fluttering like a leaf in the breeze, was Satan's tune, or so Daddy said.

I listened for a while. There was something different about the music, something tinny and brittle. It glittered in the night, closer than the stars, beckoning. I swung my leg over the far side of the wall, hopped off, and headed up the hill.

I picked my way among the trees, and the sound grew louder. When I got clear, I saw the house. It was a big, old place. What I remembered as broken down had been fixed up. The breeze blew, and I caught a whiff of cedar and sawdust.

A window, brightly lit, had been opened to let in a breeze. Under the window were some bushes. I made my way across the backyard and crouched beside them.

The sound was close but somehow far away. There was a fiddle and a guitar. The singers were men. They sang about a hammer and a drill, about steel and a worker who wanted to beat it down.

The melody twirled around my head, and somehow it mixed with Mama's song. Music seemed to be telling me something—where I came from, where I was going, or where I could escape to if I ever worked up the nerve. The music was deep and dark and mysterious. It contained answers, and I was full of questions.

When the song finished, a voice said, "That was Gid Tanner and the Skillet Lickers, singing 'John Henry.' This is the WSM Barn Dance, broadcasting from downtown Nashville, Tennessee, brought to you by the National Life and Accident Insurance Company." The man kept talking, but my mind was in the clouds above the house, over the mountains, flying west to Nashville, a place I'd heard of but had never been to.

I was listening to a radio. It sat just out of sight over

the windowsill. I knew that science had made it, like it had made the telephones and automobiles and telescopes that Mr. Wafford explained in school. Of course, science was something Daddy had no use for—didn't like it or trust it or want it around. I asked him about it once, and he just laughed.

"Science?" he said. "Why, that's just a cheap suit that Satan wears."

At the time I didn't say anything, but I wondered. In a way, wasn't science like Daddy's church? It was spirit and spark and maybe even healing, without the hocus-pocus. Science allowed you to do things. You could hear people talk and sing from miles away. You could get people excited, but not about some fever dream. This was real.

Listening in the night, I wondered what the radio looked like and what the music was saying to me. I decided to find out.

CHAPTER 4

June was hot that year. Arnie and I went barefoot and wrestled in the grass. I won, of course. Arnie didn't mind. It was something to do when school was out and we were dodging Mama and Daddy, trying to avoid chores.

The following Monday morning, Mama made pancakes. She used cornmeal and served them with honey. Pancakes meant she was in a good mood, maybe because something nice had happened or maybe just because the sun was shining.

Daddy came into the kitchen, sneaked up behind her, and kissed her neck. She laughed. I looked at Arnie and gave him a pretty good eye roll.

"It's the Lord's day," boomed Daddy, like he was preaching in the tent.

"I thought that was Saturday," said Arnie.

Daddy grinned. "Saturday's the Sabbath. Every day's the Lord's day."

Mama served the pancakes and brought out hot coffee for her and Daddy. Arnie grabbed the honey and started pouring.

"Whoa," said Mama. "Leave some for the rest of us."

Daddy pounced on his pancakes, then looked up at Arnie and me. "Good crowd Saturday night, huh? Went through a stack of communion cups. What say we form a wash brigade?"

Daddy was always forming brigades. He was at war with Satan, but also with his own odd list of taboos: dirt, sloth, fancy clothes, and anything that started with the letter *X*, which he said was godless and unnatural, such as xylophones and X-rays. When he formed brigades, I usually headed the other direction. I tried to do that after breakfast, but Daddy outsmarted me and was waiting in the backyard. He clamped a hand on the back of my neck and marched me into the tent, where Arnie was already working.

We washed communion cups, folding chairs, and a dozen other things that looked clean enough to me. It seemed that Daddy could spot dirt we never saw.

"It's the Jesus eye," he explained as we worked. "I see dirt. I see flaws. Mostly, I see sin. It's all around us, boys. Jesus hates it. He wants me to root it out."

I wondered if Jesus actually talked, and if he did, what he sounded like. Did his voice boom like Daddy's or sigh like Mama's? When he got excited, did he bark or chirp? How come he talked to Daddy but not to me?

The wash brigade took a break for lunch, then dove back in. Daddy said the folding chairs were still dirty, so Arnie and I set to work on them while he fiddled with something in back. I thought of the music I'd heard through the window and how it had made me smile.

"You know," I told Arnie as we cleaned, "singing isn't so bad. People sing in some churches."

"It's a sin," he said.

Arnie had taken to following Daddy around like a disciple. If I wanted to get Arnie's goat, I'd call him Jesus Junior.

I wiped off a chair. "Angels sing. It says so in the Bible."

Arnie kept working.

"Mama sings," I said.

He stopped and glared at me. "Liar."

"It's true."

"Mama wouldn't do that," he declared.

"I heard her. I saw her."

"I don't believe you."

I shrugged and went back to work but could tell Arnie was bothered.

Finally, he asked, "What did she sing?"

I thought of the tune and the words but didn't want to tell Arnie. Somehow it seemed private. "Just a song. I thought it was pretty."

"Don't say that."

"Why is music a sin? If you step outside the tent, lots of people sing."

Arnie shook his head, hard.

I said, "Why does Daddy hate music? Don't you think that's strange?"

"Music is bad. It's evil."

"I like it," I said.

I wondered if God was listening. For all I knew, a bolt of lightning was headed my way. I glanced at Arnie, and he fixed me with a stare. Maybe he had the Jesus eye too. When he watched me, I wondered what stains he saw, what was dirty and needed to be cleaned.

We went back to our chores. Finally, later that afternoon, Daddy inspected our work and pronounced it done. Arnie ran off to look for candy. Daddy went hunting for Mama. I checked to make sure they were gone, then made my way toward the big house.

This time, instead of climbing the hill in back, I went around the block on Taylor Street to the front of the place. It was like being in a different town. Just a block away from our little, patched-together cottage, on top of the hill, was a row of big, fancy homes. They lined Taylor and the adjacent streets, which were named for the trees that years ago had made the town wealthy and now were barely keeping it afloat—poplar, spruce, cypress.

I approached the big house, a place made of brick and stone, with a new roof and freshly painted wooden shutters. It had a circular driveway and a separate garage off to one side. There was a tall iron gate, which was odd because there was no fence, just the gate, like it was more of an idea than an actual barrier.

The gate was shut, so I walked around it. A boy my age was sitting on the front steps, looking out. He had neatly combed black hair, big ears, and a pointed nose. I studied him for a minute, then took a deep breath and ventured up the walk toward him.

He watched me all the way, and his expression never changed. His face seemed to say, *Do something. Impress me.*

"Hey," I said.

"Hey."

"You're new, aren't you?"

He nodded. "I'm Grayson Lane. People call me Gray."

Gray stuck out his hand, and I shook it. It felt good. It felt normal. Some people shake hands. Other people, like Daddy, just shake. He vibrated when the spirit took him, like he'd stuck his finger into an electrical socket. Folks loved it. They thought it showed he was filled up with God.

"Sit," said Gray. It sounded like a command, like he was used to people doing what he wanted.

I stepped forward and perched on the step beside him, wondering how long he would let me stay. I glanced around nervously. "Big porch. Big house."

He shrugged.

I said, "I'm Nate Owens."

"What do you think of this place?" he asked.

"It's beautiful," I said.

"Not the house. The town. Bristol, Tennessee. Bristol, Virginia. Whatever you call it."

"It's okay," I said.

"My father's Archibald Lane." He waited for a reaction.

"I guess I don't know who that is."

"You've heard of the Bristol Door and Lumber Company?" he asked.

"The lumber mill? Sure. My daddy used to work there. Half the town still does."

"They brought in my father to run it. That's why we're here."

I remembered overhearing my parents talk about it. According to Daddy, the lumber mill was struggling, like most businesses in town. The only ones doing well were clothing companies like Big Jack, which made overalls, and nearly all their workers were women. The lumber mill needed to turn things around, and they had hired some hotshot from Lexington to do it. I guessed Mr. Lane was the hotshot. Daddy had said something else too. I passed it along to Gray.

"I hear the lumber mill workers are starting a union," I said. "They're trying to get fair wages."

Gray looked at me. His gaze was icy. "My father can handle that."

I shivered and wondered exactly what he meant. As I

thought about it, somebody started singing. The sound was tinny and distant, like I'd heard on Saturday night, but it was a far cry from Gid Tanner and the Skillet Lickers. It sounded like what they called opera.

"Is that a radio?" I asked.

Gray smiled, and the ice melted. "Want to see it?"

"Could I?"

"Sure," he said. "Of course, there'll be an admission fee."

I stared at him, and Gray laughed. "That was a joke. Come on inside and I'll show you."

CHAPTER 5

It was a beautiful thing, made of what looked like red maple, one of the trees milled in the mountains outside Bristol. It came up to my shoulder and was polished to a sheen. At the top were some switches and a round dial with numbers. On the dial, it said Zenith. Below that was a row of curved wooden slats with fabric in between.

I'd seen a radio before, at the furniture store downtown. The store manager, Cecil McLister, had tried to sell me one. Mr. McLister knew I was only thirteen years old and was that crazy preacher's kid, but he still had tried to sell me a radio. I liked that. Of course, Daddy wouldn't have allowed me near it, but Mr. McLister didn't know that. As far as Daddy was concerned, the radio was doubly sinful: it was made by science, and music might come out.

Gray's radio was as nice as Mr. McLister's—maybe nicer. His family had put it in a sitting room at the back of the house. Next to it was the open window I had crouched below on Saturday night. A warm breeze blew in, ruffling the lace curtains.

In front of the radio sat a woman, knitting. She was pretty. Her dress was light and silky, and her hair was done up in what people called a bob. Supposedly it was the latest style, but we didn't see much of it around Bristol. I noticed that her hands were smooth and white, not rough like Mama's, though she and Mama were about the same age. I thought of Mama washing dishes and had trouble imagining this woman at the sink.

"This is my mother, Isadora Lane," Gray told me. "Mother, this is…What did you say your name was?"

"Nate Owens. Pleased to meet you, ma'am."

She cocked her head. "Owens—isn't it the preacher's name?"

"Yes, ma'am. Wilvur Owens is my father."

An unpleasant look crossed her face, like you might get if somebody had a bad rash.

"Sometimes we can hear him preaching from our house," she said. "He's got quite a voice."

I shifted uncomfortably. On the radio, the music changed. The opera stopped, and a banjo started. Mrs. Lane, who didn't seem like the banjo type, frowned and gathered up her knitting.

"I have some other things to do. It was good to meet you, Nate."

I watched her go. "Does she really like opera?"

Gray said, "In Lexington, she was chair of the Opera Guild."

"The singing sounds screechy to me. I like banjos better."
He sneered. "Hillbilly music?"

"Mountain music," I said. I had heard it in town, fiddles and harmonies drifting out of restaurants and off people's porches. The music had a rough, rugged quality, like the hills around Bristol. Sometimes, when the harmony was just right, you could hear the wind blowing through the canyons.

I approached the radio, knelt down in front of it, and listened. When the fiddling stopped, the announcer said it was somebody named Uncle Jimmy Thompson, playing with a group called the Fruit Jar Drinkers. They started another song. I liked what they were doing, even if Daddy thought it was Satan's work—or maybe because it was Satan's work. The music was rough, like Mama's hands, but it seemed simple and honest.

Besides the music, I liked the radio itself. It was parts and pieces and energy, put together to create something useful. Through it, you could overcome distance, pull in sounds through the air, and hear people singing from miles away. It wasn't magic. It wasn't wild, like church. It was science. Voices poured out based on scientific principles, laws as unbreakable as the Ten Commandments—maybe more so. Daddy would swat me if I said it, but it was true.

"What do you think?" asked Gray, beaming proudly.

"I want one," I said.

"Talk to your father."

I smiled, then saw that he was serious. My father, who

loomed so large in my life, was barely a speck in Gray's, just a voice drifting up the hill. Gray didn't seem to know about the tent or the sign, and obviously he hadn't heard about Daddy's views on music.

Thinking about it, I realized that Gray's house wasn't just on a hill. It was in a different world, where I wasn't the crazy preacher's son but could be someone new, someone of my own making. I wasn't sure yet what I thought of Gray, but I liked his house and the way it made me feel.

Gray said, "My father loves new things. When he saw this radio, he had to have it. He paid cash, and a few hours later we were listening to it right here in this room."

"Opera?" I said.

"Well, it sure wasn't hillbilly music."

"What about the WSM Barn Dance? You know, from Nashville."

Gray said, "I've listened once or twice, because WSM has the strongest signal. I don't much like it."

I heard a car, and Gray perked up.

"Dad's home," he told me. "Come on."

I followed him from the sitting room, back down the hall, and out the front door. It was a long way. If you'd gone that far at my house, you'd be standing in the middle of the street.

At one end of the circular driveway, in front of the garage, was a gleaming, green car with a long, low body and headlights shaped like drums. A man got out wearing a perfect, black suit and a fedora tilted at an angle. He had the same dark hair, big ears, and pointed nose that Gray had, or maybe it was the other way around. He pulled a leather briefcase from the car and shut the door.

"Hi, Dad," said Gray.

Mr. Lane looked up. "Oh, hello." Seeing me, he said, "Who's this?"

"He's my friend Nate," said Gray. I wasn't used to being called a friend, and it made me feel good. In town, people were more likely to giggle and whisper behind my back.

Mr. Lane held out his hand, and I shook it. His skin was soft, but his grip was hard. His fingernails were trimmed and polished.

"How's the car?" asked Gray. I noticed that he acted different with his father than with me. He seemed small and eager, like Mrs. Mim's toy poodle.

"Runs like a top," said Mr. Lane. He smiled the way Gray had smiled when he told me about the radio.

"It's beautiful," I said.

"It's a Packard 343," said Mr. Lane proudly. "Leather seats and trim, double windshield, holds seven passengers."

On the front of the hood, over the grill, was the silvery figure of a woman. She had wings and was holding a wheel in front of her.

Mr. Lane saw me looking. "They call her the Goddess of Speed," he said.

I liked the sound of that.

Gray said, "We bought this car last weekend, right off the showroom floor."

"I like machines," I said.

The words just popped out—I'm not sure why. Daddy didn't like machines, so I'd never allowed myself to think much about them. But seeing the Packard up close, I could feel its power. It shrank miles and brought people closer together. It was made for a purpose, like me. I don't mean a religious purpose, like going to heaven. I mean a purpose right here in the world, one that makes you roll up your sleeves and sweat.

"Want to see the engine?" Mr. Lane asked me.

"Could I?"

He swung open the hood, which folded back. There was a heavy metal block inside, with pipes running off of it.

"It's a straight eight," said Mr. Lane. "Three-eighty-five cubic inches. Hundred and six horsepower. Drives like a bat out of hell."

We heard a lot about hell at my house, but it was always bad. This seemed good. It seemed right and natural. I thought that if I studied Mr. Lane's car for a while and maybe laid hands on it, like Daddy did to those in his congregation, I could figure out the way it was made.

Mr. Lane closed the hood, then reached over and opened the door on the driver's side.

"Climb in," he told me.

"Really?"

"Don't ask, boy. Just do it. You may not get another chance."

I put my foot on the running board and slid behind the wheel. The leather seats swished softly. Gray opened the door on the other side and got in.

Mr. Lane pushed a button, and the engine hummed to life. In my mind, I engaged the gears and sped out the driveway, down the street, past the Bristol sign, and into the wide world.

Daddy wanted to escape the world, but I wanted to see it. When I did, I would be riding a machine like this.

Mr. Lane shut off the engine, and we followed him into the house. Gray took me up to his room. It was triple the size of mine, and the floor was a foot deep in clutter.

"Sorry about the trash," said Gray, though it didn't seem to bother him. He tromped through it like Daniel Boone in the woods.

Of course, what Gray called trash wasn't really. It was what you might get if you picked up a toy store in one hand, a five-and-dime in the other, and shook them to see what would come out. I could have spent weeks in that room. Gray, meanwhile, showed me his latest finds, which I was sure would end up on the floor in a few days.

He pulled out a baseball bat, a yo-yo, a board for Chinese checkers, and a stuffed bear that turned somersaults. What interested me the most, though, wasn't a toy but a picture.

Sticking out from some books on Gray's desk, it showed a man floating high above the trees, carried by a big, white balloon. In the distance was another man and balloon, as if traveling that way was as common as sailing a boat.

I pulled out the picture and discovered it was a magazine cover. At the top, in big, red letters, were the words *Popular Mechanics*.

"What's this?" I asked.

Gray shrugged. "It has articles about science, inventions, stuff like that."

I flipped through it. There were ads in the front:

Chemistry—Learn at Home

Boys! Electricity *is* Fun

and Pays Big Money

Following the ads were dozens of articles:

Girl Invents Airplane Motor

for Russian Government

Can Inaudible Sounds Kill?

American Inventor's Death Ray

May Spell Doom for Submarine Crews

World a Ball of Stardust, Geologist Believes

Popular Mechanics—why hadn't I heard of it before? It seemed to have been written for me.

"Could I borrow this?" I asked.

"Sure," said Gray.

He moved some things on his desk, and underneath were more of the magazines. There must have been a dozen. He organized them into a pile and plopped them into my arms.

"Don't you want these?" I asked.

"I get a new one every month," he said. "I can't keep up. Anyway, think of it as a public service. You're helping to clean my room."

A few minutes later, I headed home for supper with a stack of magazines tucked under my arm. The hills around town were turning orange and pink. The tree branches criss-crossed above me, like highways on a map.

Two nights before, I had heard sounds through a window. Now, in the pages of a magazine, the window had become a door. On the other side were the outlines of something big and new. It could have been science or escape or maybe hope—hope for a world that made sense, where if you had a problem, you could fix it instead of pray about it. That world had radios and cars and balloons. The door was open. Somehow, in spite of Daddy, I was going to step through.

CHAPTER 6

I saw Gray the next day. I saw a lot of him that summer. Looking back on it, I realize we always went to his house. I knew his parents, but he didn't know mine. Every once in a while, he'd make a joke about the tent and the preacher. I might agree with what he said, but I didn't like him saying it.

At Gray's house, we would listen to his radio. At the end of the day, Gray's father would pull into the driveway in his Packard. One day in late June, when he got out of the car, he went straight to the hood and opened it. He leaned in and studied the engine. We were watching from the house and decided to investigate.

When we approached, he told us, "The engine's missing."

Gray said, "But…it's right here."

Mr. Lane glanced at me, and I smiled.

"He means one of the cylinders isn't firing," I explained. "There's an ignition problem, because a cylinder isn't getting fuel or it's lost compression."

"How did you know that?" asked Mr. Lane.

"*Popular Mechanics*. I read it all the time."

"Do you know how to fix it?"

I leaned down and checked the engine. "Well, sir, one article had some suggestions. Could you start the engine, please?"

Gray stared at me the way you'd watch some strange animal at the zoo—maybe a wombat or a three-toed sloth. For a minute, Mr. Lane stared too. Then he got in and switched on the ignition. The big engine fired up, but the sound was rough.

There were eight cylinders, and as I went down the row, I disconnected the spark plug wires one at a time, the way the article had suggested. Most of them caused the engine to sound worse, but when I got near the end of the row, the sound didn't change.

"This is the one," I said.

"How do you know?" asked Gray.

"This cylinder was already misfiring. That's why there was no change."

I connected the spark plug wire, and this time I wiggled it to make sure it was in place. The engine smoothed out and sounded like I'd heard it that very first day.

Mr. Gray revved the engine, then turned it off and climbed out of the car.

"What did you say your name was?" he asked.

"Nate, sir. Nate Owens."

Mr. Lane turned to his son. "This boy's smart."

"Uh, yes, sir," answered Gray, like he was surprised to say it.

"Nate," said Mr. Lane, "can I come to you if there are more problems?"

"Sure, if you think I can help," I said. "I'm new at this. But I could try."

From then on, when Mr. Lane came home, he would always call me by name. If he had questions about his car, he'd ask me. Most of the time I was able to help. If I didn't know the answer, I'd go to *Popular Mechanics* or the library and find out. Of course, when he had real problems he got them fixed in town, but he seemed to like getting help from me. Maybe it was because my advice was free.

***

Gray could be a jerk sometimes, but I enjoyed going to his house. If you liked science, there wasn't a better place in town. Mr. Lane wanted all the latest things, and he had the money to buy them.

There was the radio, of course, and the car. Besides those, the house was filled with gadgets, all of which Gray was happy to demonstrate. A contraption called a vacuum cleaner sucked dirt from the carpets. Instead of an icebox, they had an electric refrigerator. There was a special light-weight iron that I'd never seen Mrs. Lane use.

Best of all was the toaster. You put in two slices of bread, and a minute later, they'd pop up, ready to butter. Gray and I felt it was important to test various kinds of bread. We didn't eat them all, but the toaster worked just fine.

One afternoon in July when I went to see him, Gray met me at the front door, waving our local newspaper, the *Herald Courier.*

"Look at this!" he said, tapping the paper with his finger.

He had folded the paper back to an ad in the first section. It showed a picture of a woman listening to something that looked like a radio but wasn't.

I studied the ad. "Victrolas—I've heard of those."

I had just read an article about them in *Popular Mechanics*. They played music on black shellac disks called records. But Victrolas had seemed like something from the future. Now they were in Bristol, at a furniture store downtown.

"Let's go," said Gray. "If it looks good, maybe my father will buy one."

We headed downtown with a purpose, walking west on State Street under the Bristol sign and past the train station, the Wood-Nickels Department Store, the barber shop, and Woolworth's Five-and-Dime.

The Clark-Jones-Sheeley Company, one of the oldest furniture stores in Bristol, was between Sixth and Seventh. Clark, Jones, and Sheeley might have been old-fashioned, but Cecil McLister wasn't. Whenever Mama and I passed by, he tried to pull us in and show us the latest products. He had sold a lot of radios, and now it looked like he was pushing Victrolas.

When Gray and I went inside, he came hurrying up to us.

"Welcome, boys," he said, beaming. "So, Gray, how do you like your radio?"

"Just fine, sir," said Gray. He dug out the newspaper and pointed to the ad. "Can we see that Victrola?"

"Absolutely. Amazing machine, and a beautiful piece of furniture. It's made by the Victor Talking Machine Company in Camden, New Jersey."

He led us to a display at the front of the store where three of the machines were lined up.

"Technically these are gramophones," he said, "but Victor calls theirs the Victrola. Here's the one you want."

He pointed to the biggest of the three. It was a wooden cabinet that came up to my chest, with doors on the front that had carved designs. On the right side was a handle, like you might find on an ice-cream maker.

Mr. McLister noticed Gray eyeing the handle and said, "Go ahead, son. Give it a crank."

Gray cranked, and a man's voice sang out:

> Ain't she sweet? See her walking
> down that street.
> Yes, I ask you very confidentially,
> ain't she sweet?

Mr. McLister turned to me. "Brand-new record. Just got it in. What do you think?"

I heard Daddy's voice in my head, railing about music. "I like it," I said.

Gray examined the Victrola. "Is this like a radio?"

Mr. McLister chuckled. "Not even close."

He opened a door on the front of the cabinet. Inside was a round platform about a foot wide, and turning on top of it was the black disk they called a record. A metal arm went out over the record. Mr. McLister lifted the arm and showed us a needle at the end.

"See this needle? When the record goes around, it follows the grooves and vibrates, and then the vibrations are amplified electronically into sounds."

I said, "The sounds are carved into the record? In those grooves?"

Mr. McLister nodded. "Technology—don't you love it?"

"Can I see the record?" I asked him.

"You bet."

Mr. McLister set down the metal arm, stopped the record, lifted it out of the cabinet, and handed it to me. In the middle of the record was a hole, and around that was a printed label with a picture of a dog listening to a gramophone.

Victor
"Ain't She Sweet"
Gene Austin
With Nat Shilkret and His Orchestra

"Victor makes records too?" I asked him.

"You bet. It helps them sell Victrolas. They do popular music, symphonies, operas. Just recently they hired a new man, Ralph Peer, who thinks they can sell records to everyday folks—blues, polkas, even mountain music like we have around here."

I held the record up to the light so I could see the grooves. It looked like there were hundreds of them, carved in perfect circles. Then I realized something and laughed.

"What's so funny?" asked Gray.

"You see all these grooves? It looks like there's a lot of them, right?"

"So?"

"It's really just one," I told him.

He studied the record. "What are you talking about?"

"Don't you see? It's a single groove, starting at the outside and going around and around until it reaches the middle."

Mr. McLister took the record back, smiling. "He's right, Gray. It's one long, long groove."

"And the music is carved into it," I said.

Somehow Gene Austin, Nat Shilkret, and everyone in the orchestra were in that groove. It was science, but it also seemed like magic.

Gray stepped back and admired the Victrola. "I like this one. I'll ask my father if we can get it."

Mr. McLister nodded. "Tell him to call me, and I'll have it delivered."

I was still thinking about that long, long groove.

"Do you have some of those other records?" I asked.

"Sure." He opened the side of the cabinet and showed us a stack of records, each in a white paper sleeve. "I usually throw in a few of these with every purchase of a Victrola. If

Gray and his father buy one, they can pick out some records to take home."

Gray lifted out the stack. I gazed over his shoulder as he flipped through the records: "Stardust," "Me and My Shadow," "My Blue Heaven."

Looking at the records, I had a sudden thought. "This Victrola plays the records. But how do they make them?"

"You can find out for yourself," he said. "Ralph Peer is coming to town on Friday. He's looking for songs to put on records, and he thinks our mountain folks might have some."

I thought of Mama's song. "He'll be here?" I asked.

Mr. McLister smiled. "He's bringing some machines and equipment. And you can bet he'll be carving some grooves."

CHAPTER 7

It was a car Mr. Lane would have been proud to drive.

I found out later it was a Cadillac Series 314-A, but all I knew then was that it was beautiful. It was two-toned, with a maroon body and a black roof. There was a long hood, and running boards swooped over the wheels. Like the Packard, it had a silvery hood ornament, but instead of the Goddess of Speed, this one had wings and a temperature gauge to tell you if the car was overheating.

I had checked around and found out that the people from Victor would be staying at the Palace Hotel, on Front Street across from the train station. It was an impressive place, with a barber shop, billiard room, and restaurant.

On Friday I hung around in front, and sure enough, late that afternoon, two cars approached, and one of them was the Cadillac. I knew it was them because the cars had New Jersey license plates.

The Cadillac parked in front and out stepped a man as fancy as the car. He was big, with a broad chest and an expression on his face that was all business. He wore a pinstriped suit and tie, with a vest and shiny gold cuff links. His hair was slicked back, and the crease on his pants was sharp as a knife. He was rich, I could tell, but not like Mr. Lane. This man had more than money. The difference was hard to describe. Maybe it was style or the way he carried himself.

I watched as the man went around to the other side of the Cadillac and opened the door for his passenger. A woman stepped out, wearing jewelry and a black dress that must have been silk. Her hair was done up in a bob, and her face glowed. She took the man's arm, and as they walked toward the hotel, she seemed to float.

When they went inside, the second car pulled up. It was an old Ford. I wondered where the recording machine was, and I figured it wasn't in the Cadillac. That left the Ford. I noticed that the car's body was sitting low over the wheels, which meant it might be carrying something heavy.

Two men climbed out with their sleeves rolled up. The shirts were wrinkled and smudged, as if the men had been working or were expecting to. One man was tall and stern looking. The other was short and pudgy, with a shy smile. He reminded me of Mr. Fowler at church. I wondered if he barked.

The tall man glanced at the hotel, then looked up and down Front Street. He shook his head and murmured something to the other one, who laughed. When they headed for the lobby, I casually walked over to the Ford and peered inside. In the back seat were several big, boxy shapes that were covered with a blanket.

"Hey!" someone yelled.

I looked up and saw the tall man striding toward me.

"Get away from there!" he said.

"I was just curious—"

"Curiosity killed the cat."

I'd heard Daddy say the same thing. What cat? What were they talking about?

"Now scram!" the man told me. He pulled some keys from his pocket, locked the car doors, shot me another look, then went back inside.

I walked off toward the train station as if I were leaving, then ducked inside and waited. When the couple came back out, I checked to make sure the coast was clear, then approached the man in the suit.

I had no idea what to say. Finally some words popped out.

"Welcome to Bristol!"

The man turned and saw me. The woman did too.

She chuckled and asked, "Who are you? The chamber of commerce?"

"I'm Nate Owens," I said.

To my surprise, the man offered his hand. I didn't know what else to do, so I shook it.

"Pleased to meet you, Nate," he said. "I'm Ralph Peer, and this is Mrs. Peer."

I nodded. "Mr. McLister said you'd be here."

The man said, "Cecil McLister? You know him?"

"Yes, sir. He said you'd be coming from the Victor Talking Machine Company to make some records."

"McLister's a good man. He arranged the sessions for us. We'll set up this weekend, then start recording on Monday."

"Where?" I asked.

He pulled a slip of paper from his pocket and checked it. "The Taylor-Christian Hat Company, 408 State Street."

Just then the lobby door opened, and the two men came out. They spotted me, and the tall one came hurrying up.

"Hey, I told you to leave!" He turned to the man in the suit. "Sorry, Ralph. I'll take care of him."

"It's all right," said Peer. "We were just talking. Gentlemen, this is my friend Nate Owens. Nate, these are our two sound engineers, Edward Crabtree and Fred Holt. The tall one is Crabtree. He keeps a close eye on the equipment."

Crabtree shuffled his feet and nodded.

Peer said, "Nate here knows Cecil. I told him about the sessions."

Daddy says ask and it shall be given. I figured I'd give it a try.

"I was wondering about those sessions," I said. "You think I could come?"

The short man, Holt, exchanged looks with Peer. Crabtree frowned.

"Do you realize how delicate a recording is?" said Crabtree. "The slightest noise can ruin it—a sniffle, a sneeze, a squeaky floorboard. If we let you come, we'll have to let everybody, and believe me, they'll ask."

Peer thought for a minute. "Sorry, son, but he's right. We've come a long way for this. I'd like to say yes, but we need to do our work."

Mrs. Peer eyed me. "Still, you might be able to help."

"How?" I asked.

"That was a long, dusty road. We'd like something to drink."

I said, "They have Coca-Colas at Bunting's Drug Store, up the street. Milkshakes too."

"I was thinking of something a little stronger," she said.

A voice piped up from behind me. "Try Crystal Caverns."

I turned and saw a girl. I wondered how long she'd been standing there and how much she had heard. She was my age—short and thin, with a quick smile; curly, red hair; and bright-green eyes. She wore a simple print dress and boots, as if her body were soft and her feet were tough. In the curls of her hair was a ribbon that was green like her eyes.

She gazed at me, as if challenging me to say something, then turned back to Mrs. Peer. "There's a restaurant, but I hear they also have drinks. It's down Highway 421, a few miles south of town."

I had heard Mama and Daddy talk about alcohol, and in church, Daddy called it "the devil's potion." It was illegal to buy because of the Prohibition laws, but I'd noticed that Gray's family kept bottles of it in the cupboard. Mrs. Lane liked to carry a glass of it around the house, and Mr. Lane usually had a sip when he got home from work. Even Gray said he had tried it. Once he had mentioned Crystal Caverns, the place where his parents bought the stuff. He called it a speakeasy.

I studied the red-haired girl. How did she know about it?

Mrs. Peer smiled at her husband. "I like this girl."

Reaching into his pocket, Peer pulled out a silver dollar.

"That's for you," he told the girl.

She took the coin. "Thank you, sir."

Peer and his wife headed for the Cadillac. I said, "Are you really looking for songs?"

He paused. "Yes, I am."

"I might have one," I told him.

"What about singers?" asked the girl. "I'm a singer."

Peer said, "Singers, songs—that's why we're here."

"Come on, Ralph," said his wife. "I'm thirsty."

He shot us a grin, then walked her to the Cadillac and they drove off. Crabtree and Holt pulled their bags from the trunk and went inside. The girl watched them. I watched her.

"Who are you?" I asked.

"I saw you in church," she said. "Mama wanted to go. Somebody told her the preacher puts on a good show."

"He's my father, you know."

"That's what I hear," she said. "So, what are you going to do? Jump around like he does? Yell about Jesus?"

"No."

"Do you believe all that stuff?" she asked.

"I'm not sure," I said.

"That means you don't."

I said, "I believe in science."

She nodded. "I'm Sue Dean Baker."

"Nate Owens."

"I know," she said.

"So, what about you? What are you doing here?"

"It's a free country."

"I didn't mean it that way. I was just curious."

Sue Dean shrugged, then glanced up at me. "I work here sometimes. I help clean rooms."

She seemed uncomfortable admitting it. I tried to put her at ease. "I do some cleaning. Folding chairs. Communion cups. You know, the family business."

"Is that what it is?"

"Daddy says it's a holy calling. I say it puts food on the table."

Sue Dean glanced at her watch. "That's what I need to do. Put food on the table. My parents get off work soon."

She started off down the street, then turned back. "See you there?"

"Where?"

"The Taylor-Christian Hat Company. Monday morning."

CHAPTER 8

Ralph Peer and his friends would be setting up their recording machines that weekend, so I tried to slip away Saturday morning to watch them. Daddy caught me though. He put me on a work brigade with Arnie, where our job was to figure out what a new altar might look like. Daddy said it shouldn't be too fancy, as if we were putting on airs, but it couldn't be too plain either. After all, it was for the living God. Daddy sent us to the shed behind our house, where he kept some tools along with other odds and ends.

Arnie thought a soapbox might work. He had heard about people doing all kinds of things with a soapbox, such as slapping wheels on it and racing in it, which he desperately wanted to try. He said an altar might be the closest he'd get to doing that. The altar wouldn't have wheels, but maybe, if conditions were right and Mr. Fowler started to bark, Jesus would lift it up and fly it to heaven.

"You really believe that?" I asked him.

Arnie picked up an old soapbox, brushed it off, and held it out at arm's length.

"Sure," he said, eyeing the box. "Don't you?"

I sighed and helped him with the altar. After sanding and a coat of paint, it actually looked pretty good. We took it to show Daddy and heard him rustling around in the bushes outside the tent.

"Lord Jesus!" we heard him say.

Arnie and I glanced at each other.

"Daddy, you okay?" called Arnie.

He came out from the bushes a minute later holding a snake that must have been four feet long. He gripped it behind the head so it wouldn't bite him. The snake was a beautiful tan color, with dark-brown markings like coffee stains. It wriggled in his hand.

"Will you look at this?" exclaimed Daddy. "It's a timber rattler!"

"Wow," breathed Arnie.

"Be careful!" I said.

"Careful?" said Daddy. "Was Jesus careful? Did he back off from the lepers? Did he run from those Roman soldiers?"

"That thing is poisonous," I said.

Daddy grinned. "Check your Bible, Son. Mark 16:18. 'They shall take up serpents; and if they drink any deadly thing, it shall not hurt them; they shall lay hands on the sick, and they shall recover.'"

Daddy made me nervous when he talked like that. When he quoted weird Bible verses, you never knew what would come next.

"What are you going to do with it?" I asked.

"Maybe we should name it," he said.

The snake gave off an angry rattle, and Daddy grinned. "Beelzebub, how's that?"

Arnie perked up. "Isn't that the devil's name?"

"Bingo!" said Daddy. "It's another name for Satan. I'll shut Beelzebub in a box, then pray about him. Then maybe some Saturday night, when the spirit is sagging, I'll pull him out to liven things up."

"Would you?" said Arnie. He bit his lip and his eyes danced. I couldn't tell if he was scared or excited.

Daddy spent the rest of the morning in the shed, and when he came out, Mama yelled at him. She usually supported Daddy's projects, but not this one. It brought me up short to hear her talk to him like that. She ordered him to box up that snake and never let it out, then informed Arnie and me that if we went anywhere near it, she'd tan our hides.

The sun beat down hard that day, and the heat lingered into the night, especially inside the tent. But that didn't keep the people away. They came like always, looking for miracles or maybe just for something to do.

That night, Daddy preached like nobody's business. He once told me he never knew what he'd say till he got up there and looked in people's eyes. Then he saw what they needed and would dive right in. He cooked up his sermons the way you'd make a casserole for a church supper, using leftovers and pieces of this and that. This week, one of the pieces was Beelzebub.

He eyed the people, then suddenly exclaimed, "You ever think about snakes?"

Next to me, Mama tensed up. "Dear Lord," she breathed.

Arnie sat up straight. His eyes glowed, and he started breathing hard, a little bit like he'd done at the Strand Theater downtown when we slipped in the back door and saw *Flesh and the Devil* with Miss Greta Garbo.

Daddy whipped off his coat and tie. Rolling up his sleeves, he paced back and forth, agitated. "Scientists tell us that snakes are reptiles, just another kind of animal like rabbits and birds. But we know the truth, don't we? They're evil. They're captains of sin, scum of the earth, Satan's cheerleaders. They crawl on their bellies. Did you know they used to walk? That's right. Before the Garden, before Adam and Eve, snakes pranced around like you and me."

"Show us, Preacher!" somebody shouted.

Daddy grinned and demonstrated. He jumped, wiggled, and squirmed. Of course, he was careful not to dance, because that would be a sin.

"Then one day, it all changed," said Daddy. "A snake tempted Eve. When he was caught, his legs withered up and blew away like dead leaves. Ever since, snakes have slithered around on their bellies."

Next to me, Mama wrung her hands. Earlier that day, following her orders, Daddy had shut the snake in a box, then built a cage for it on top of a worktable. Daddy called his cage "the snake pit" and had put Beelzebub inside while she had watched. But I knew, just as sure as the world, that one of these days Daddy would open that cage. I wondered if it would be tonight.

Daddy pulled a handkerchief from his back pocket and wiped off his forehead. He cleared his throat. He clapped his hands the way he did sometimes to get his blood flowing. He looked over at Mama. Then he shouted "Amen!" and moved on from snakes to other signs of the devil, such as music. It appeared we were safe from Beelzebub, at least for another week.

Later in the service, when it came time for the offering, Daddy stepped up to the new altar. People had no way of knowing that the back of the altar said *Ivory Soap*.

"My boy Arnie made this," Daddy announced. "Arnie, come say hi to the folks."

Arnie, sitting beside me on the front row, hopped up and joined Daddy at the altar.

"What do you say?" Daddy asked him.

"Give to Jesus!" said Arnie.

Daddy passed the offering plate. The crowd must have liked Arnie, because the plate was full by the time it reached us.

Looking down at it, I thought of Sue Dean and wondered what she would think. Maybe this was the family business. Maybe it was just a show. Maybe we really were crazy.

I passed the plate. The walls closed in.

CHAPTER 9

I woke up early Monday morning and lay in bed, thinking. In just a few hours, Ralph Peer and his friends would be working their magic, and I needed it. They would be looking for songs, and I had one. But there was a problem.

I wanted to be there for all of it, but I couldn't spend that much time downtown without Daddy noticing and hearing that it involved music.

So I made up a story. Old Mrs. Rickover was a member of Daddy's church, and it seemed that she needed my help with spring cleaning. Conveniently, the job would start that day and would take a week or two.

The great thing about my story was that Mrs. Rickover was forgetful. In fact, *forgetful* was a mild term for it. She needed directions to find the bathroom, and once a month or so, she would put up Christmas decorations. If Daddy asked her about spring cleaning and she didn't remember it, he would just shrug and figure she had forgotten.

When I told Daddy about the job, he said, "She's not paying you, is she?"

"Uh, no, sir."

He nodded, pleased. "'Heal the sick, raise the dead, cleanse lepers, cast out demons. You received without paying; give without pay.' Matthew 10:8."

"Actually," I said, "we'll just be cleaning the house."

That morning I set out for Mrs. Rickover's place, then hung a left and headed downtown, where Cecil McLister had rented space in the old Taylor-Christian Hat Company building, on the Tennessee side of State Street, within sight of the train station. The hat store had been closed for years, so the first floor was dark, but I saw lights and activity on in the second floor. I knew Crabtree and Holt must be inside, because the Ford was parked in front.

Someone else was parked in front too. It was Sue Dean, sitting on the curb and holding a couple of sweet rolls. She got to her feet and handed me one.

"I stopped by Hecht's Bakery, over on Shelby Street."

"Is this for me?" I said.

"You don't have to eat it. If you're not interested, I'll have both of them."

"I'm interested."

I accepted the sweet roll and took a bite. In my planning, the one thing I'd forgotten was breakfast.

"I saw them go inside," she said. "You know, those two sound engineers."

"Did they say anything?"

"'Out of my way, missy!'"

I smiled. "That sounds like Crabtree."

We heard voices and turned to see Ralph Peer and Cecil McLister approach from the direction of the hotel. Peer looked as elegant as ever, with a starched collar and tie. Mr. McLister, wearing a straw hat, was nibbling on a toothpick. He saw me and grinned.

"Well, well," he said. "Ralph told me you were at the hotel last Friday. Back again today?"

"Yes, sir. I'd like to help."

Peer spotted Sue Dean. "You helped us Friday night. Thanks to you, Mrs. Peer and I didn't go thirsty."

"What about today?" I asked. "We're good workers."

Peer shook his head. "I'm afraid not. Recording is a delicate business."

"I could sing," said Sue Dean.

McLister chuckled. "That's what they all say."

The men swept past us. I watched them go into the building and up the stairs.

Sue Dean sat back down on the curb, and I took a spot next to her. As we ate our sweet rolls, a thought struck me.

"You know that book *The Wonderful Wizard of Oz*?" I asked Sue Dean.

She nodded. "Mama used to read it to me at bedtime."

"I liked the part where they went to see the Wizard," I said. "They all wanted something different—courage, brains, a heart."

"Don't forget home. That's what Dorothy wanted."

I thought of Ralph Peer, in his fancy suit and expensive car.

"If you saw the Wizard," I said, "what would you ask for?"

"I guess I'm like Dorothy. I'd ask for home—not just a house, but a place where Mama, Daddy, and I could all be happy."

"Aren't they happy now?"

"They're tired," she said. "They're worried, so they fight. Half the time they aren't even home because they're working."

"Are you happy?"

"I'd like to be," she said.

She blinked a couple of times, then looked up at me. "How about you? If you saw the Wizard, what would you ask for?"

I considered it for a minute. "I'd ask him to put me together."

"Put you together?"

"See this street? One side is Tennessee, the other's Virginia. Bristol's split in two. Sometimes that's the way I feel. Half of me is in that tent, listening to Daddy preach. The other half is off somewhere, doing all the things I'm not allowed to do."

"Like what?" she asked.

"Music. Science. Daddy says they're sins."

Sue Dean gazed at me as if she was trying to see inside.

"You told Mr. Peer you might have a song," she said. "What did you mean?"

I had never told anyone, but suddenly I wanted Sue Dean to know. "It's Mama's song. When she thinks nobody's there, she hums it. Sometimes I catch a few words. I asked her about it once, and she got the most terrible look on her face. Like she was frightened and angry all at the same time."

"Could I hear it?"

"I'm not much of a singer."

"I don't care."

I closed my eyes and imagined Mama that night, singing in the kitchen. I hummed along, then sang the words. It was strange and a little bit frightening to release my secret into the world. I sang four lines, then stopped where Mama did.

"Have you heard that before?" I asked.

"No. But it's lovely."

"I think it's important," I said, "but I don't know why."

Sue Dean nodded gravely, then sat back down on the curb. I joined her. We worked on our sweet rolls for a while. I noticed she had icing on her chin, and I wiped it off. She blushed.

Sitting next to the Ford, we watched Crabtree and Holt make several trips there to get some things. It seemed like the car was a kind of traveling tool chest. On one of his trips, Crabtree spotted us and pointed.

"Stay back," he said. "I'm watching you."

I caught Sue Dean's eye, and she smiled.

Around eight o'clock, a beat-up Model T came slowly down the street. The driver stuck his head out the window and looked around. When he saw the hat company building, he said something to the people in the car, then pulled in.

The door opened, and the driver got out. He was a thin man about Daddy's age, wearing a white hat and a wrinkled suit.

"Is this the recording place?" he asked us.

"Yes, sir," I said. "Mr. Peer is up on the second floor."

"Who are you?"

"An assistant. Can I carry something for you?"

Just then the other car doors swung open. A woman got out on the passenger side, and two men unfolded themselves from the back seat. All of them looked like they were dressed up for Sunday school.

"Much obliged," said the driver, "but we can handle it."

"Are you a singer?" asked Sue Dean.

He grinned. "Yes, ma'am. Course, I also play a few instruments—guitar, autoharp, clawhammer banjo. Give it to me, I'll play it." The man stuck out his hand.

Sue Dean shook it, and so did I.

"Name's Ernest Stoneman," he said, "but they call me Pop. This is my wife Hattie, and those two men are Kahle Brewer and Ralph Mooney. We're from Galax, Virginia."

The two men nodded, then started pulling instruments out of the car. There were enough to supply a marching band.

Hattie picked up one, the others each took an armful, and they headed into the building and up the stairs.

Sue Dean glanced at me. "So you're an assistant?"

"First you say it, then you do it. That's what Daddy tells me."

"You're saying it, I'll give you that."

I wanted to assist, but frankly there wasn't much need of it. A little while later, one or two other singers came by carrying instrument cases and disappeared into the building. Meanwhile, Sue Dean and I sat on the curb.

She told me about her mom and dad, Harley and Carleen, who along with Sue Dean had recently moved to town from Lynchburg, Virginia, across the state border. Her dad needed work and had found it at Bristol Door and Lumber, the company where Gray's father worked.

"Have you heard of Archibald Lane?" I asked.

She frowned. "Daddy says he's an awful person. He'll fire you if you look at him wrong. He's cracking down on the union."

The union was a big topic in town. Organizers had come through the lumber companies, trying to sign people up, claiming they could get them better hours and higher wages.

"Daddy's pro-union, of course," she went on. "He tells stories about goons roaming through the yard, watching for union members, carrying out midnight beatings."

"If your father doesn't like it, why doesn't he leave?" I asked.

She stared at me like I'd come from the planet Mars. "Have you lived your whole life inside that church tent? It's tough out here. People are losing jobs. If you have one, you hang on to it, even if you hate your boss."

I pictured Mr. Lane in his neatly pressed suit, perfect car, and fancy house. I wondered if he knew about those goons and what they were doing. I thought of Gray and decided not to mention him to Sue Dean.

She looked off into the trees. "Daddy works all the time. We don't see much of him. When he comes home, he just falls asleep. Mama takes in ironing. She gets lonely. Truth is, that's why we went to church. She wasn't looking to be saved. She just wanted to see some people."

It must have been warm inside the building, because every once in a while somebody on the second floor would open a window and we'd hear a few snatches of music, as if the players were rehearsing. Then they'd close the window and we couldn't hear a thing.

Later on, Sue Dean brought pimento cheese sandwiches from her house and we sat some more. Mr. Peer had said he was looking for singers and songs, and we wanted to provide them. But really, I'm not sure what we were waiting for. It just felt like something important could happen, and I wanted to be there. Most of all, I wanted to get inside.

Tuesday was the same but different. For one thing I was by myself, because Sue Dean had things to do at home. I asked Gray to come, but he wasn't interested. Some musi-cians showed up and climbed the stairs, the same as Monday. This time, though, they were part of a gospel group, Ernest Phipps and His Holiness Singers. For the three hundred and fifteenth time, I tried to figure out why Daddy hated music and didn't allow it in his church. If holiness could be sung, the way Ernest Phipps did, wouldn't God listen? Wouldn't God jump up and dance, if he ever did such things?

The next day, Wednesday, started out pretty much the same. I headed off to Mrs. Rickover's house, then detoured downtown. Ernest Stoneman showed up again, and later there was a group called the Blue Ridge Corn Shuckers. Then something happened, and everything changed—for me, for Sue Dean, and for Bristol.

PART II

SUNSHINE IN THE SHADOWS

There is sunshine in the shadows
There is sunshine in the rain
There is sunshine in our sorrows
Though our hearts are filled with pain

—A. P. Carter, "Sunshine in the Shadows"

CHAPTER 10

I saw it in the *Bristol News Bulletin* on Wednesday evening. It was just a few sentences, but they caused an explosion.

I didn't know it at the time, but by the third day, Ralph Peer had been getting frustrated because there weren't many singers to record. Cecil McLister told him the key was publicity, and McLister invited a reporter to the Wednesday morning sessions. The reporter listened to Ernest Stoneman, then visited with Peer.

I saw the reporter when he came out of the building, so I knew something was up. I checked the paper that night and was able to read about what I hadn't been allowed to see. An article described Ralph Peer and what he was doing. It mentioned the room and how it was draped with blankets to muffle outside sounds. Mostly it talked about the singers and how Peer was holding auditions to get more of them.

At the end of the article was the paragraph that caused all the fuss. It was about Ernest Stoneman and His Dixie Mountaineers, the people we had met two days earlier. Singers around town read the article and told their friends, and their friends told *their* friends, and by the end of the week, every-one was talking about it.

> The quartette costs the Victor company close to $200 a day—Stoneman receiving $100, and each of his assistants $25. Stoneman is regarded as one of the finest banjoists in the country, his numbers selling rapidly. He is a carpenter and song leader at Galax. He received from the company $3,600 last year as his share of the proceeds on his records.

You have to understand—mountain people don't have much money. When they heard that someone was making $25 or $100 or, by God, $3,600 just to sing, they lit up like bulbs in the Bristol sign. After reading the article, singers for miles around packed their bags and headed to Bristol.

***

They started coming that weekend—in cars and wagons, on horseback and on foot. They carried their instruments in cases, in burlap bags, or just slung over their shoulders. They brought their bands and families, and it seemed that all of them wanted to stay at Mrs. Pierce's boardinghouse, on the Virginia side of State Street. Mr. Pierce was a barber, and he was happy to give people a trim before their auditions.

It was exciting, but it made me nervous too. Up to then, Daddy didn't know what was going on at the hat company, and now he did. There was music happening, so you could bet he'd be on it like a pointer on a dead bird, which would make it harder for me to stick to my story. I might even have to spend some time at Mrs. Rickover's house.

Sure enough, Daddy heard about the music and sprang into action. He painted some signs inviting people to church, and on Saturday morning, Arnie and I posted the signs around the boardinghouse and down the block. That night the tent was crowded with visitors.

"Welcome, Satan!" boomed Daddy from the pulpit.

The people, confused, whispered and buzzed.

"You heard me," said Daddy. "Satan's here. You brought him!"

Daddy stepped out from behind the soapbox pulpit and pointed into the crowd. "You! You! You dragged him in here with your music. You stink of it. You reek of it. Music! The devil's tune. Satan's melody. That guitar you play? A pitchfork! That big ol' string bass? A coffin! Death is coming. He's blowing his whistle. You're humming along. You're on the devil's railroad.

"But look here—on the tracks ahead, a lone figure. Sandals set. Robe blowing in the wind. Face just glowing. It's Jesus! Look out, engineer. Look out, musicians. Throw down that banjo. Stomp it. Crush it to pieces. Grind it to dust."

Next to me, Arnie beamed. I wondered what visions swirled in his head and whether they involved a snake. Me? I squirmed, desperate to leave the tent. Hot air bore down on me. Daddy's words pinned me down. I must have groaned, because Mama leaned over and put her arm around me.

Daddy wouldn't stop. He knew the place was full of musicians, and he didn't pause for a minute. You could call it bravery, I guess, or maybe it was a death wish. I imagined some stranger in the third row charging the pulpit, flailing his mandolin, and beating Daddy to a pulp.

The thought scared me, but it wouldn't go away. That was the thing about Daddy's sermons. Whether or not you agreed with him, they grabbed you by the shoulders, shook you hard, and wouldn't let go. Colors were brighter. Pictures flashed by like dreams.

Maybe that was his real talent. Not preaching or praying, but making you feel—taking an ordinary summer night and filling it with joy and fear and dread. I wondered where he learned that. Did he practice, or did it grow wild, like mushrooms in a dark cave?

It ended finally. I watched the people file out and wondered what the musicians were thinking. Maybe somebody was converted. Maybe a guitar was burned or a banjo stomped. Or maybe they just enjoyed the excitement, and they'd go on playing and singing and then come back for more.

The next day, inspired by the big turnout, Daddy painted more signs. The first Wednesday of the month was that week, which meant there would be a potluck at church with a bonus sermon from Daddy, and he wanted to make sure the visitors heard it.

Arnie and I spent an hour tacking up more signs around town, and when Arnie finished, I noticed him sneaking off. I followed, curious, and was surprised when he went to our house. He didn't go inside though. Instead he circled around back and entered the shed.

I moved to a window, and through the dirt and cobwebs, I watched Arnie approach the worktable where Beelzebub was coiled inside his cage. Arnie stood there, staring like he was in some kind of trance. He smiled vaguely and reached for the cage door.

Beelzebub saw Arnie, and his eyes glowed. Through the window I heard a faint sound.

The rattler was rattling.

I shook my head, as if I'd been in a trance of my own. Racing to the front of the shed, I plunged inside.

"Arnie!"

He reached for the cage door, barely an inch from Beelzebub. As he touched the door, I tackled him. We went down in a heap. Beelzebub, rattling furiously, hurled himself against the side of the cage. Four feet long and fat from the mice Daddy had fed him, Beelzebub struck repeatedly, but all he got was wire.

I held Arnie down, afraid he was going to try it again. "What do you think you're doing?"

"He's beautiful," said Arnie, gazing up at the cage.

"He's death! And if he doesn't kill you, Mama will."

"What about danger?" asked Arnie.

"What about it?"

"It's what Daddy preaches. Danger. Living on the edge. That's where Jesus lives."

"Jesus said to love your neighbor, not snakes."

Arnie peered up at the cage, then back at me. His eyes glinted like sparks from flint. "Jesus loves all kinds of things. Even you. Even me."

I had watched Arnie grow up in Daddy's tent, but until that moment I don't think I realized what it had done to him. He was like clay, and Daddy had molded him into something dark and odd. He was Daddy distilled, Daddy twisted.

He said, "You won't tell them, will you?"

"Mama and Daddy? I don't know."

I tried to imagine what I'd say. *Your son is warped.* If I told them, I wondered how they would feel. Hurt. Puzzled. Angry, probably at me.

I sighed. "Okay, I won't tell. But you've got to promise. Stay away from that snake, you hear?"

He nodded, and I let him up. He brushed off his clothes, and we left the shed without another word.

CHAPTER 11

On Monday morning I headed off in the general direction of Mrs. Rickover's house. On the way I met Sue Dean, and we joined the crowd of people going to the Taylor-Christian building for auditions. At first I kept glancing around, worried that I'd be recognized by church members. I didn't see any, and after a while I relaxed, figuring music auditions were the last place I'd find them.

Sue Dean wore a dress she'd borrowed from her mother's closet after her parents had gone off to work.

"You look nice," I said. "Really nice."

She reached out and straightened my collar.

"You too," she said.

"I guess you read that article in the paper."

She nodded. "I'm going to audition for Mr. Peer. What about you?"

"I thought I'd sing Mama's song, or what I know of it. Maybe somebody will recognize it and tell me more."

Sue Dean cocked her head and gave me a little smile. "You're not a good singer."

I laughed. "Okay, you're right. But what am I supposed to do?"

"Could I sing it?" she asked.

"Mama's song? For the audition?"

"Why not? I have other songs too, but I could start with yours. We could go in together. If anybody knows the song, you'll find out."

"All right," I said. "Sure."

I was glad, but I was nervous. Mama's song, which seemed so private, would be out in the world.

When we reached the building, the line stretched out the front door and into the street. Sue Dean stood in line, while I went to Hecht's Bakery to buy a sweet roll for us to split.

When I got back, she was talking to some people in line behind her. A tall, gangly man had slicked-down hair and eyes that blazed. The two women with him looked like sisters, plain faced but handsome. Behind them was a little girl who held a baby in her arms.

When Sue Dean saw me, she said, "Nate, they're from Poor Valley!"

"Where's that?" I asked.

"Scott County, Virginia, thirty miles across the border. It's not far from Lynchburg, where I'm from."

"We came by car and felt every bump," said one of the women, smiling. She was the older of the two but couldn't have been more than thirty.

"Nate," said Sue Dean, "this is Sara Carter. That's her husband, A.P., and her cousin Maybelle. Maybelle's married to A.P.'s brother Eck, so she's also Sara's sister-in-law."

"Confusing, isn't it?" said Sara. "Sometimes I get mixed up myself."

Maybelle shot us a shy grin. She shifted uncomfortably, and I noticed for the first time that she was pregnant, and pretty far along at that.

"Pleased to meet you," I said. I stuck out my hand and realized there was a sweet roll in it.

"Oops," I said. I broke the roll in two and handed half to Sue Dean.

The baby let out a howl.

"That's little Joe," Sara told us, taking the baby from the girl and putting him on her shoulder. "He's still nursing, so we brought him with us. This here's Gladys, my eight-year-old. She came along to babysit while we sing. Isn't that right, sugar?"

Gladys nodded. She was a tiny thing. It was a wonder she was able to hold Joe, who looked as big for his age as she was little.

"Where are you staying?" asked Sue Dean.

"A.P.'s sister lives in town. You might know her—Virgie Hobbs? Her husband is Roy."

"Sure," I said. "They come to our church."

"So, you two sing?" Sara asked us.

"Sue Dean does," I said. "How about you all? Are you singers?"

She nodded. "I do the melody. Maybelle sings harmony. A.P. chimes in with bass."

"We love the old songs," said Maybelle.

"Old but new," said A.P.

His voice had a tremor, and so did his hands. He shifted restlessly from foot to foot. In all the time I knew him, then and later, I'm not sure he ever got comfortable. He would fidget and squirm, scratch and wheeze. He reminded me of a hound dog, circling round and round, looking for a good place to lie down and never quite finding it.

He said, "You take an old song, tuck it, trim it, then lay it out flat like a napkin on the table. It's old but new."

Sue Dean noticed the battered cases beside Sara and Maybelle.

"Are those your instruments?" she asked.

Sara nodded. "Mine's an autoharp. But Maybelle's—that's the one."

"I play the guitar," said Maybelle.

"Her brothers got it when she was thirteen," Sara told us, "and she picked it up quicker than they did. Never took lessons, so she made her own way of playing—chords and melodies all at the same time. Scratch, she calls it. Sounds like two players, not one."

I studied the young pregnant woman and didn't see

anything special about her. I guess talent shows up in all kinds of ways.

"Where do you play?" Sue Dean asked.

"Schools and churches mostly," said Sara. "Fifteen cents a head. On a good night, we might make twenty-five dollars. On a bad night, we might cover the cost of gas."

A.P.'s hands stabbed the air, and his voice quivered. "Not like this Stoneman fella—one hundred dollars a day, three thousand a year. We could do that. Yes, sir."

"We tried out for a record once before," Sara told us proudly. "It was last year, with the Brunswick Record Company. We auditioned at Kingsport. They turned us down though."

"They wanted a fiddler," declared A.P. "Well, I'm a fiddler, but I told them we were a group. Songs, voices, guitar—that's what we do."

"So we came home," said Sara. "A.P. went back to his day jobs—working the sawmill, selling fruit trees. It's a good life."

"Not as good as music," said A.P.

Sara's eyes sparkled. "When he proposed, A.P. said he loved me. Personally, I think what he loved was my voice."

A.P. ducked his head and hummed, as if somewhere inside his head, he was listening to a song.

I thought about the song in my head, the one I'd heard in the darkness and had carried with me ever since. It still was there, and I wondered where it came from.

I asked A.P., "You know lots of songs, right?"

"A few," he said.

Sara snorted. "A few thousand."

"I heard a song once," I told him. "Maybe you know it."

I thought of Mama in the kitchen, singing as she baked. I remembered some bits of melody and words, and I sang them as best I could.

"Keep going," said A.P., listening intently.

"That's all I have."

"It's a good song," said A.P., "but I don't know it."

Sue Dean squeezed my hand, and the line started moving. We talked some more, and Sue Dean tried holding the baby. The minute she took him, he stopped crying.

Gladys grinned up at her. "I think he likes you."

Sue Dean held Joe for a while longer, then visited with Sara. Maybelle took out her guitar, tuned it, and strummed a few chords. Meanwhile A.P. fidgeted, and I found myself doing the same. After all, this was Oz, and we were about to see the Wizard.

CHAPTER 12

The line was like a river, flowing down the stairs, out the door, and around the bend. We moved upstream and finally reached the bottom of the stairs. At the top was a door. I wondered what was inside.

The building was hot, and I was sweating. The door at the top of the stairs was like a ribbon at the finish line. As we got near, there was a commotion down below.

"Coming through!" someone said. "Let me through."

The voice sounded familiar, and when I turned around I saw why. Gray was pushing his way through the crowd. I was surprised because the week before, when I had asked him to come with me to the building, he had just laughed.

"It's hillbilly music," he had said. "Why would I be interested in that?"

Now, seeing all the people, he had apparently changed his mind.

"I hate him," said Sue Dean.

Her anger didn't surprise me. I guess it was why I hadn't told her I knew Gray. He was in a different part of my life from Sue Dean—separated, like Daddy and Mr. Peer, like church and the wide world. I lived my life in boxes.

Sue Dean glared as Gray approached. She murmured, "They say his son is stuck up, like no one is good enough for him."

I turned away so Gray wouldn't notice me, but not fast enough.

"Nate!" he said. "What are you doing here?"

I glanced at Sue Dean. She was staring at me.

"Hello," I said.

Gray saw Sue Dean, and his expression brightened. Obviously he didn't notice that she was mad. I guess he wasn't the most observant guy in town.

"Who's your friend?" Gray asked me.

"Sue Dean Baker," she said. "My father works at the lumber mill. His name's Harley Baker."

Gray shrugged. "Sorry. Never heard of him."

"You will," she said.

Gray turned back to me. "Do you sing?"

"Not really."

Sue Dean watched us. "You know each other?"

"Are you kidding?" said Gray. "He's my best friend. Right, Nate?"

I wasn't sure what to say. My boxes were collapsing, breaking apart and bleeding into each other.

"Why are you here?" I asked finally.

"The man from Victor sounds important," said Gray, eyeing Sue Dean. "I thought I should meet him."

"Good luck if you don't sing," said Sue Dean. "Nate tried all last week and couldn't get in."

Gray chuckled. "All due respect, I might have more luck than Nate."

For the first time, I saw Gray through Sue Dean's eyes. He might be smiling, but suddenly he seemed foolish.

"Go ahead and try," I said. "All they can do is throw you out."

Gray laughed and chucked me on the arm. "Yeah right. See you later."

He nodded to Sue Dean, then headed up the stairs, pushing and elbowing people as he went.

Sue Dean watched me, disappointed. I hadn't exactly lied to her, but I hadn't told her the truth either.

Gray reached the top of the stairs and barged through the door. I heard voices inside, and Edward Crabtree appeared, gripping Gray by the arm and marching him down. As they went past, Gray said, "You can't do this! I'll tell my father!"

Sue Dean caught my eye and held it. I wondered if things would ever be the same. Then, out of the blue, she started to giggle. I laughed too, and then we were howling. If you can laugh with somebody, maybe things aren't so bad.

We got to the top of the stairs, and a few minutes later they motioned us in.

I thought of Mama's song and gulped. "Here goes."

It was a big room, taking up most of the second floor. In the days of the hat company, it must have been used for storage, because it had a high ceiling and a bare wooden floor. I was surprised at how dark it was, then realized why. The windows were covered with blankets to keep out noise.

I squinted in the darkness. In the middle of the room they had set up a table and four chairs, where Ralph Peer and his wife sat. He leaned back with his legs crossed, and she was taking notes on a clipboard. Next to them was Fred Holt, thumbing through a magazine. The empty chair must have been where Crabtree had been sitting. I had to admit I was glad he wasn't there.

As I watched, Peer said something to Holt, and Holt nodded. Setting down his magazine, he made his way across the room to an area where blankets had been hung from the ceiling. He ducked behind one of them, and I saw a flash of metal. It was the recording machine. It had to be.

"Next," called Peer.

As we approached the table, he studied me.

"You," he said.

I shrugged. "Welcome to Bristol."

Mrs. Peer smiled at Sue Dean. "We went back to Crystal Caverns. That's some place."

"You're a singer?" Peer asked me. "Why didn't you say so?"

"Actually, sir, I don't sing. But my friend does. Her name is Sue Dean Baker."

He grinned. "What are you, her agent?"

I wasn't sure what an agent was, but it sounded all right to me.

"I guess so," I said.

Peer turned to Sue Dean and looked her over. "Where's your instrument? Where's the band?"

"I sing by myself," she said.

Mrs. Peer glanced at her husband, then looked at Sue Dean. "Sweetheart, singing by yourself is fine, but I'm afraid it's not what Mr. Peer's looking for."

"She's really good," I said.

"I'm sorry," said Mrs. Peer.

"Next," her husband called.

Just like that, our time was up. Our chance was gone. Peer and his wife turned away. There was nothing to do but leave.

Just then, a loud screech came from the open doorway. Either someone was torturing a chicken, or little Joe was crying again.

Sara came through the door, holding Joe. His face was red, and he was screaming bloody murder.

"Great," muttered Peer.

Maybelle followed. A.P. tottered along behind, with Gladys holding his hand.

I started to leave, but Sue Dean had other ideas. She went

up to Sara and took the baby, who immediately stopped crying. Sue Dean smiled at Gladys.

"Mommy and Daddy are going to sing," she said. "Let's go over here and listen."

Sue Dean led Gladys off to the side, rocking Joe all the while.

"Well, what do you know," said Peer.

The Carters got out their instruments. Sue Dean held the baby. Peer settled back in the chair, and his wife picked up her clipboard.

Somewhere off in a distant corner of the sky, the sun peeked out from behind a cloud. The tiniest sliver of light fell across the floor, leading away from the table and the singers, toward a part of the room that was hidden by a blanket.

It was time to look behind the curtain.

CHAPTER 13

While Peer watched the Carters, I slipped behind him and made my way to the other side of the room. I glanced around nervously, then took a deep breath and ducked behind the blanket.

"You're persistent, aren't you?"

I looked up and saw Fred Holt, the other sound engineer. Where Crabtree was tall, Holt was short. Where Crabtree was stern, Holt was soft-spoken and friendly. He was smiling now.

"Yes, sir," I said. "I guess so."

I looked past him to a stack of equipment that took up most of the space behind the blanket. I guess I was staring, because Holt chuckled.

"You like it?"

I liked shoes. I liked chewing gum. This was way past like. It was a whole new territory, sprung off the pages of *Popular Mechanics* and into the world.

I moved toward the equipment, then hesitated.

"Can I?" I asked.

He stepped aside and held out his arm like the ringmaster

at a circus. I touched one of the machines. Made of metal, it was hard and cold.

I said, "Are you recording today?"

"Maybe this afternoon," he said. "This morning is just auditions. Ralph's trying to find more singers."

I ran my hand along the side of the machine. "How does it work?"

"You really want to know?"

"Yes."

He looked over the equipment with an easy glance, the way I might check my bike before hopping on.

"It's an electronic process," he said. "Recording used to be acoustic. The singers would shout into a big horn to catch the sound, and it didn't work very well. Then Western Electric developed this."

He nodded toward a strange-looking contraption. It was a metal pole shaped something like a hat rack, but instead of hooks at the top, there was a round, metal disk the size of a large biscuit, maybe an inch thick in the middle and tapering to half of that at the edges. It was covered with round holes—a big one circled by a ring of smaller ones—with fabric behind the openings.

"They call it a microphone," said Holt. "It changes sound vibrations into an electric current."

I gazed at the microphone. It gleamed silver in the dim light, like something mailed from the future.

Holt motioned toward the machine that rested beside it, the one I'd run my hand along. "That's the amplifier. It takes the signal from the microphone and boosts the power. Then the signal is fed into the last part of the system, the lathe."

He moved to the lathe, a metal box with a round platform on top. It reminded me of the Victrola that Cecil McLister had shown us that day at the store but bulkier and made of solid metal. Jutting out over the platform was a metal arm with a needle on the end. Beneath it, resting on the platform, was a disk that appeared to be made of soft wax.

"Is that a record?" I asked.

"It's a record master, or will be. The signal comes from the amp and goes to this arm. See that needle on the end? It's called a stylus. It cuts a groove into the wax to create the master. From the master, they make a metal stamper that's used to press records. The records are identical to the master, except they're made out of shellac, so they'll be strong and hard."

I looked back at the microphone and imagined people singing into it. Their voices would be converted into an electronic signal, boosted by the amplifier, captured on the master, and pressed onto records, ready to be played by people like Grayson Lane.

The equipment was like a rocket ship and a time machine all rolled into one. People could sing in one place and be heard halfway around the world, a hundred years from now.

Holt said, "The old acoustic recorders were big and

couldn't be moved. Electronic equipment is different. The machines are smaller. You can load them into a car and take them anyplace there's electricity—even Bristol, Tennessee."

He paused, grinning. That's when the angels started to sing.

My heart is sad and I'm in sorrow,
>
for the only one I love
>
When shall I see him, oh, no, never,
>
till I meet him in heaven above

Holt looked at me with his head kind of sideways, like he was listening hard. Then he pulled back the blanket.

It turned out to be one angel, Sara Carter. Next to her, Maybelle stitched the melody with her guitar. A.P. chimed in every so often with a musical grunt.

The Carters had set up in front of the table, and they were deep into the music. It was just an audition, not a recording session, but there was something about the way they played that made you stop and listen.

The song was about a woman whose man didn't love her anymore. Because of it, she was ready to die and be buried under a weeping willow tree. The words were sad, but the music was sadder. You could hear the woman's pain in Sara's voice and Maybelle's strumming. It was there, in between the notes. But there was something else. It was in everything the

Carters sang, then and later—a spirit, a strength, a feeling that, whatever happened, they would carry on and be all right.

"My goodness," murmured Holt.

When the song was over, A.P. turned to Ralph Peer. "Want to hear another one?"

I noticed that Peer wasn't leaning back anymore. He was sitting up straight in his chair. Next to him, Mrs. Peer was taking notes like mad.

"How many do you have?" Peer asked him.

"How many do you want?" A.P. said.

Peer said, "Can you come back tonight? I'd like to record a few."

A.P.'s lip twitched, which I found out later was as close as he got to a smile.

"Name a time," he said.

Mrs. Peer glanced at her clipboard. "How about six thirty?"

A.P. nodded, and that was that.

Sara, her eyes gleaming, hugged Maybelle and then hurried across the room, where she kissed Gladys and pinched the baby's cheek. A.P. and Maybelle gathered up their things, and I figured it was time to go.

"Thanks for showing me the equipment," I told Holt. "You think I could come back?"

He glanced around the room, as if he was looking for Crabtree.

"Sure," he said. "That'd be fine."

I shot him a quick grin, then hurried off after the Carters and Sue Dean.

I caught them at the top of the stairs. Sara had Gladys by the hand, and Sue Dean held Joe, who had fallen asleep. Maybelle was close by. A.P. stood next to her, but he was already far away, probably thinking of more songs.

"You did it!" I said.

Sara ducked her head, but there was no covering up that smile. Maybelle looked over at Sue Dean and Joe.

"How'd you get him to sleep?" Maybelle asked her.

"It was the music," said Sue Dean. "When he heard Sara's voice, he nodded off."

"Can you help us again tonight?" asked Sara. "We don't want a baby crying on our records."

Sue Dean glanced at me. "I think so. I'll try."

"Mr. Peer liked your song," I told them.

"So did I," said Sue Dean. "It sounded like the music I hear in my dreams."

I looked beyond the Carters to the other singers, in line to the bottom of the stairs and beyond. I wondered how many would be invited back like the Carters and how many would go home and do their singing around the kitchen table.

Sue Dean and I followed the Carters down the stairs, past the singers, and out of the building. The Carters headed off, looking for lunch.

"I should get going," said Sue Dean. "See you tonight?"

"I'll be there," I told her.

She nodded, then walked off toward home. I watched her go, thinking of the way her cheeks turned pink when she smiled.

"Hello, Nate," someone said behind me.

I turned around. Arnie was standing there.

CHAPTER 14

"How are those chores coming?" asked Arnie. "You know, the ones you've been doing for Mrs. Rickover."

"Fine," I said.

"Liar."

His eyes were bright. His voice was pinched, like something was pressing down on it. "I checked around. You haven't been at Mrs. Rickover's. You've been here."

I'd been careful but not careful enough. Then I wondered why I should have to be careful at all. I'd spent the day in a place that stretched out to the horizon and beyond, a place where the only things that mattered were imagination and talent. Compared to that, the world I lived in—with its rules and walls and boxes—seemed all wrong.

"Everyone else has been here too," I said, nodding toward the line of singers. "This is important, Arnie. It's big. Don't you see?"

"It's music, the devil's tune. I know it. You know it. And you lied to get it."

I studied him. It seemed like I'd been doing it a lot recently.

"What's wrong with you?" I asked.

Arnie spoke again, like he was spitting. "That's Satan talking. You know what the Bible says. 'When he lies, he speaks his native language, for he is a liar and the father of lies.' John 8:44."

"You're a kid," I said. "You used to laugh and play jacks."

He blinked, and for just a moment, I saw my little brother.

"This is serious, Nate. It's your soul. I'll have to tell Mama and Daddy what you've been doing."

I tried to imagine how Daddy would react. Yell. Preach. Accuse me of music, the worst sin of all. For sure I'd be grounded. I wouldn't be able to hear the Carters sing that night. I might never see Ralph Peer and his machines again. I couldn't let that happen.

"No, you won't tell Mama and Daddy," I said. "Because if you do, I'll tell them what you were doing."

He stared at me blankly for a moment.

"The snake," I said. "Beelzebub."

As he realized what I was saying, Arnie began to struggle and fidget, like he was tied up with rope and wanted desperately to get loose.

"I mean it, Arnie. Keep quiet about the music, or I'll tell them."

Arnie looked at the hat company building and the line of people coming out the door.

"It's not right," he said. "It's a sin."

I thought of Daddy railing against music. There was fire in Daddy's eyes, but as I watched him in my mind, I saw something else too. It was fear. He was as frightened of music as Mama was scared of that snake. I wondered why. Whatever the reason, their fears had collided, balanced out, and stopped Arnie—at least for now.

I went back to the hat company that night. Arnie watched me leave, his face dark, but didn't say anything. When I got to town, the auditions were over, and the line of singers was gone, scattered across the countryside. The Carters were the only ones left, waiting in front of the building with Sue Dean. It turned out that A.P. had rehearsed them all afternoon. They had worked up four or five songs, then had come back for their appointment.

"My fingers are all plucked out," Maybelle told us.

"Sprout another set," said A.P.

Sue Dean asked, "Where are Mr. Peer and the others?"

"Supper break," answered Sara. "They auditioned all morning and recorded all afternoon. We met the last group coming out. They called themselves the Bull Mountain Moonshiners. Swear to goodness, with the names of those bands, you'd think all we ever do around here is drink hooch."

There was a noise behind us, and the Cadillac pulled up. As Peer and his friends got out of the car, little Joe let out a wail, and Gladys tried to comfort him. Crabtree and Holt exchanged nervous glances.

"Hey, Ralph," said Crabtree, "those kids aren't going up-stairs, are they? The microphone's pretty sensitive."

Peer turned to his wife. "Can you help us out?"

Now Mrs. Peer was the one who looked nervous. "Me? I don't know anything about babies."

"Well, do something." Peer took out his wallet and handed her a couple of dollars. "Here, buy them some ice cream."

Sue Dean took the baby, and he stopped squalling.

"Ice cream sounds great," said Sue Dean. "Sara, you go with the others. Come on, Gladys. What flavor do you like?"

Mrs. Peer joined them, and they headed off to the soda shop just a few doors down.

Peer fished in his pocket, pulled out a key, and unlocked the building's front door. It seemed strange, since nobody in Bristol locked anything. Peer led the way upstairs, followed by his two engineers and the Carters. I stayed close behind Sara, Maybelle, and A.P. When Crabtree spotted me, Sara told him, "He's with us."

"He's a kid," said Crabtree.

"I'm their agent," I said.

Peer chuckled. Crabtree muttered something. Upstairs, he went to the microphone, which had been moved from be-hind the curtain to the middle of the room. He fiddled with it and turned to the Carters.

"Sing into this," he said. "Don't shout. Use your normal voices."

He tapped the microphone, then he and Holt moved across the room to the blanket and stepped behind it. I imagined the amplifier and lathe back there, plugged in and ready to go.

Peer sat behind the table again while the Carters got ready. Sara unpacked her autoharp, an instrument halfway between a banjo and a kitchen drawer. It had strings you played and buttons you pushed. Maybelle pulled out her guitar, wiped it lovingly with a smooth cloth, and they tuned up. A.P. lurked behind them, like Father Time.

"What do you have for us?" asked Peer.

A.P. cleared his throat. "Thought we'd start with the song we did this morning, 'Bury Me under the Weeping Willow.'"

It wasn't a grunt or a word or a phrase. It was an actual sentence. As I came to learn later, A.P. said the most when he was talking about songs.

"That's fine, fine," said Peer. "Let's cut it."

It made me think of scissors. Then I remembered the lathe, poised above the wax disk, ready to cut a groove into it. You sang a song. You played a guitar. You cut a record.

Peer called out toward the blanket, "Ready, boys?"

Crabtree called back, "Have them sing a few notes. We'll do a check."

Sara sang a phrase or two, and apparently there was a problem with the equipment.

"Give us a minute," said Crabtree.

Peer got up and chatted with the Carters, which gave me a chance to duck behind the blanket.

I found Crabtree and Holt bent over the amplifier. They had removed the cover and were fooling with the wires. Nearby were two sets of earphones.

Crabtree glanced up. "What are you doing here?"

Holt said, "He's okay."

Crabtree blinked and turned back to the amp. I had assumed Crabtree was in charge, but suddenly, I wondered. Maybe Holt led quietly, the way A.P. led the Carters.

Holt found the problem, a loose wire at the back. He tightened it up and replaced the cover. The two of them put on the earphones.

Crabtree called out, "Have them try again."

Sara sang a phrase, and Holt nodded.

"We're ready," called Crabtree.

"All right," said Peer. "Quiet, everybody."

Holt started the lathe. The disk turned. The needle dropped. Crabtree reached through the blanket and signaled. The Carters sang.

A groove appeared behind the needle, starting at the edge and tracing a perfect circle around the wax disk. The needle completed the circle and started a second one just inside the first, then another, then another. In front of the needle was a smooth, flat surface; behind the needle was life, carved into the disk.

I knew from an article in *Popular Mechanics* that if you looked at the groove through a microscope, you'd see a canyon with dips and bumps and steep edges. They were Sara's voice and autoharp. They were Maybelle's guitar.

I wondered how a shape could be a sound, a sound could tell a story, and a story could bring people living and breathing into the room. It was happening in that building that used to be a hat shop, and I was there. In the song, a woman stood before me, weeping. The willow tree slumped. A cold breeze blew through the branches.

I glanced at Holt. He pressed the earphones to his head. He looked up at me and held my gaze. He had flipped the switches and gotten everything ready, and now all he could do was "witness," as Daddy would say—stay still and soak it in and notice every little thing, because the needle is carving and the disk is turning, and the trip around is so very short.

Then it was over. The Carters finished their song, and the needle was lifted. The disk wasn't smooth anymore. It was a master, and soon it would be a record. Sara and Maybelle and A.P. were singing in those grooves, and I liked to think that, somehow, I was in there with them.

They recorded three more songs that night: "Little Log Cabin by the Sea," "The Poor Orphan Child," and "The Storms Are on the Ocean." Holt would put a new disk on the lathe. Peer would nod. A.P. would count them off, and the Carters would sing. They told about love and loss, despair and hope. People entered the room in those songs. The place was crowded with them.

Peer wanted more, so he invited the Carters back the next morning. Sue Dean and I were there. For some reason, A.P. didn't show up. I pictured him wandering the hills, humming softly to himself. But Sara and Maybelle came, and by that time, Peer knew they were the ones who made the music. When they arrived, Sue Dean took the children downstairs again, where Mrs. Peer kept them supplied with ice cream.

The Carters recorded two more songs, "Single Girl, Married Girl" and "The Wandering Boy." Without A.P., there was something pure and beautiful about the music—two women telling stories in songs. Maybe A.P. had sensed it, and that's why he had stayed away.

Years later, when people talked about what happened at Bristol, they called it an explosion—the big bang of country music. From what I saw, it wasn't like that. It was quiet, then there was music, then it was quiet again. Peer and his workers went about their business, and the singers went about theirs—the Carter Family, Jimmie Rodgers, Ernest Stoneman, and a dozen others. The room came alive, and because of science, it was preserved for people to witness. That's all it was, but it turned out to be everything.

CHAPTER 15

"So long," said Sara. "Thank you for helping us."

She smiled at me and embraced Sue Dean.

"Do you have to go?" I asked.

They had finished their recording session just a few hours earlier. I didn't want it to end, ever. But there we were, saying goodbye to the Carters. Sue Dean kissed the baby. Maybelle and Gladys hugged us. A.P. nodded stiffly.

They climbed into their car, a plain, black four-door Essex that belonged to Maybelle's husband, Eck. Eck had lent A.P. the car but had told him they were crazy to drive all over creation to sing a few songs. A.P. had the last laugh though. Before leaving, he had pulled me aside and shown me what Ralph Peer had given him after the sessions: six crisp fifty-dollar bills, one for each song.

"There's more where that came from," declared A.P. "Mr. Peer says he'll pay us fifty dollars for every song we bring him, plus royalties if we write them."

"What are royalties?" I asked.

"If the records sell, we get a little bit of the money. You

know, a percentage."

To me, the money was almost as amazing as the recording machines. I knew men who worked all day for a dollar, and the Carters had made three hundred just for singing.

Sue Dean and I watched as the Essex pulled away and slowly drove off down State Street, taking the Carters back home. They waved, then turned the corner and were gone.

"I miss them already," said Sue Dean, staring after the car. "I love that little baby. Gladys too."

I nodded. I missed Sara's voice and Maybelle's guitar. I missed the way A.P. showed up in the songs, like a stranger who had stumbled into the room. Years ago, Sister had left. Now the Carters. Mama said leaving was a part of life, but I didn't like it.

"I'd better get home," said Sue Dean. "I've been neglecting my chores."

She headed off down the street. I had things to do at home too, but I wasn't ready for them. They were part of my old life. I had a new life now, or a glimpse of one. It sparkled in the distance, like the silver microphone.

A few minutes after the Carters left, Peer and his friends arrived, just returning from lunch.

"Need some help?" I asked Holt.

Crabtree snorted, but Holt nodded. "Come on in."

That day I watched as they recorded more musicians. Henry Whitter, a harmonica player from Virginia, sang about a fox hunt. The Shelor Family did "Big Bend Gal" and three other tunes. Mr. and Mrs. J. W. Baker told a sad story in "The Newmarket Wreck," about a train accident near Knoxville.

Afterward I helped Holt and Crabtree clean up. With all the assisting I'd been doing, I had worked up an appetite, so I headed home and found Mama in the kitchen.

I gave her a peck on the cheek. "What's for supper?"

"Your daddy wants to see you. He's in the shed."

"Playing with the snake?" I joked.

She fixed me with a look. "It's serious, Nate."

My stomach did a little flip. I crossed the kitchen, pushed open the screen door, and made the long walk to the shed.

Daddy was there, all right. He wasn't playing with the snake though. Beelzebub was in his cage. Daddy was sitting in an old wooden chair, staring at him.

"Hello, Son," said Daddy. He kept studying that snake, as if the answer to his problems were spelled out on its back.

Beelzebub must have spotted me, because he rattled furiously and hurled himself against the side of the cage.

I jumped back. "Can't we get rid of that thing?"

"I like it," said Daddy. "So does Arnie."

Arnie had been spending time with Beelzebub, but Daddy wasn't supposed to know it. I glanced over at Daddy, wondering how he knew.

He said, "Arnie came to me this morning. Admitted he's been sneaking out here against his mother's wishes, watching Beelzebub and then lying about it."

I sighed. "So he decided to confess."

"Repent," said Daddy. "The word is *repent*. It's what you do when you've sinned." His gaze bore into me, like one of the drills at the lumber mill.

I looked away.

"Arnie's a good boy," said Daddy. "Sometimes he sins. I do too. So do you." He cocked his head and waited.

"What do you want me to say?" I asked finally.

"Forgive me, Lord."

"For what?" I said. "Covering up for Arnie?"

"I know what you've been doing. Arnie told me."

I clenched my fists. My fingernails cut into my palms. "What did he say?"

Daddy's face had turned red, and one eye twitched. He tried to look calm, but it was like clamping a lid on a boiling kettle.

"I'd like you to say it," he told me.

"Why are you asking if he already told you?"

"Say it."

A feeling built up inside my chest, then exploded like a hand grenade. "Music. Music, okay? Are you happy?"

"What about it?"

I thought I'd feel bad when I said it, but I didn't. I felt good. I felt strong. I took a deep breath, and the words just flowed.

"I like music. So does everybody. They hear it on the

radio. They play it on records. That's where I've been—not with Mrs. Rickover, but at the old hat company downtown. A man's there from Camden, New Jersey, and he's making records. Wonderful records. Records with music. You were wrong, Daddy. It's not Satan. In fact, I think it may be God."

Daddy slapped me across the face. "Blasphemy!" he thundered.

He had never hit me before. It hurt bad, and not just because of the pain.

"Down on your knees, Son," he growled, pushing me to the floor. I tried to push back, but he was too strong. My knees hit the floor, scraping the old boards.

"Why are you like this?" I asked. "Why do you hate music?"

His face was all contorted. "Forgive me, Lord. I hit my son." He squeezed my shoulders, hard. "Now you."

"Ow! What! What do you want me to do?"

"Repent, sinner!"

Once, long ago, I loved my daddy. He was big and loud and wild. But that was over. It had been over for a long time. He always said the devil was his enemy. Now Daddy was mine. He stood between me and my dreams, and there seemed to be no way around.

I pushed away his hands and struggled to my feet. "This is crazy," I said. "This whole thing. We're headed somewhere bad, and I don't like it."

"Repent!" said Daddy.

"I'm sorry I lied to you. I'm sorry I sneaked around. But I'm not sorry I heard the music. Daddy, it was beautiful."

He closed his eyes and shook his head. "Get thee behind me, Satan."

"Satan's got nothing to do with it! He's not in me or that snake, and he's not in the music. Why do you keep talking about him?"

Daddy blinked a few times, then looked at me, almost like he was pleading. "He's real. I feel him. I see him every day."

"Where?"

"Everywhere."

He was quiet, but I think his head was filled with voices—shouting, screaming, begging. I felt sorry for him...until he spoke.

"You're not going back," he told me.

"To the recording sessions? I have to. I'm helping them."

"You'll be at home all week. Thinking about what you did. Repenting."

"I can't go out?"

"You'll go to church. That's all."

He turned to leave.

"Daddy—"

"That's it. I'm not changing my mind."

He walked out of the shed and slammed the door.

CHAPTER 16

It just about killed me.

Not the showdown with Daddy, though that still made me mad. The hard part was thinking about Peer and his friends going on without me. The auditions were over, and recording sessions were scheduled all week. They were carving grooves, and I was cleaning my room, helping my mother, staring at the walls. I pictured myself in wonderful scenes—listening to new singers, operating the machines, working in Camden, New Jersey, with an office next to Ralph Peer.

Daddy preached his bonus sermon Wednesday night, and attendance was light. I was there, because it was my one chance to get out of the house. Sitting in the tent, I remembered the signs Arnie and I had posted around town advertising the Wednesday night service. Turned out we'd been wasting our time, because most of the folks who had come to audition were long gone, headed back home with their music.

At times that night it felt like Daddy was preaching straight at me, the way you'd load a rifle and aim it. It was all about music and Satan, but to tell you the truth, I didn't hear much of it. I was back at the hat company, listening to the Carters.

Sue Dean stopped by that night after the service. She had worked at the hotel that day, and afterward, dropping by the sessions, she'd been surprised I wasn't there and had decided to check on me. She found me sitting on the front porch, and I told her what had happened.

"You're grounded all week?" she said. "That's serious."

"Music is a serious sin. The worst. He would have let me off easy if I'd just killed someone."

"Why is he like that?" she asked.

"I wish I knew. Just thinking about music sets him off. You should have heard him. But you know what was strange? Deep down, it almost seemed that he was mad at himself. All the yelling, the punishment—like it was for him as much as me. So why do I have to suffer?"

"My father gets mad sometimes," said Sue Dean. "Usually it's about union stuff. He said work is getting dangerous. He calls it a war."

I snorted. "His war, his music. Why do we have to worry about our parents' problems? We've got enough of our own."

Sue Dean looked at me, surprised. "Nate, it's family."

"Yeah, I guess."

What was family? Memories. Rules. Fragments of a song. A mystery.

"Did you see Mr. Peer?" I asked

"No, but I did talk to that engineer. The nice one."

"Mr. Holt."

"He showed me the recording schedule. Nate, they finish on Friday. You're going to miss it all."

So that was it. The end of my big adventure.

The moon was out that night. It lit up her face and the trees and some clouds over the mountains. It was a wide world, but mine was getting narrower by the day.

Sue Dean went on home, leaving me with my thoughts. After Friday, Peer and his friends would pack up their things and go. They would float off like those clouds, disappear into the ether, and I'd never see them again.

The thoughts were eating me alive. They gnawed all day Thursday and Friday. By Saturday morning I'd had enough. The world was moving on, and I was missing out.

It was time to do something.

Getting dressed, I checked the hallway, opened my bedroom window, and climbed out. I made my way down the street, going from tree to tree to stay out of sight. When I reached the end of the block, I took off running. Downtown was straight ahead. The hat company loomed in the distance like a beacon, like Oz.

When I got there, I glanced around, looking for Ralph Peer. As I did, Holt and Crabtree pulled up in their Ford.

"Morning," said Holt, wearing a wry grin. "Want to help?"

He and Crabtree were headed for the stairs with their sleeves rolled up, like they were ready to work.

"Yes, sir," I said.

Packing was harder than I expected. The equipment had to be taken apart and put into special boxes. Crabtree was in charge of the packing. He seemed to do better with nuts and bolts than with people. Finally, a little before lunch, we loaded the boxes into the Ford.

Holt wiped his forehead with a handkerchief and grinned at me. "You enjoy this, don't you?"

"Yes, sir."

"I've noticed you want to learn. That's good."

Beside him, Crabtree mumbled something.

"Pardon me?" I said.

Crabtree said, "You're all right, kid."

He was still mumbling, but that time I had heard him loud and clear.

"Is Mr. Peer around?" I asked.

I rode with them to the hotel. I sat in the back seat of the Ford, next to the boxes of equipment that were covered with blankets, like that first day. Resting my hand on top of one, I thought of what was inside and wondered if I'd see it again.

At the hotel, Peer and his wife were just coming out through the lobby door. Behind them, a bellman struggled with their bags, finally loading them into the back of their Cadillac. Peer peeled off a dollar and gave it to him.

"Thank you for your help," Mrs. Peer told him, smiling warmly.

The bellman tipped his cap and gazed at her. Unfortunately, he also kept walking and tripped over the curb. "Fine, fine," he said. He straightened up and then disappeared into the lobby, dripping mud.

Peer opened the car door for his wife, then came around to the driver's side.

"Sir?" I said.

He looked up. "Oh, hello. It's Nate, isn't it?"

"Yes, sir. I wonder if we could talk for a second."

"About what?"

I had rehearsed the moment over and over in my head, but when it came, I found myself struggling for words.

"Well, sir, I enjoyed working with you—you know, helping out. I was just wondering, you think I could help again?"

"Sorry, Nate, but we're leaving."

"I mean somewhere else. Not Bristol. Where are you going next?"

He gave me a funny look. "Charleston, Savannah."

My future stretched out before me, in Charleston and beyond. I had to grab it.

"I'll come with you," I blurted. "I can help with the equipment. I'll do whatever you need. I'm good with machines."

He laughed, then caught himself. "You're serious."

"Yes, sir."

"I'm afraid that's impossible. My goodness, you're only—what? Twelve years old?"

My face burned. "Thirteen."

"Don't you see?"

"I'm good. I'm a hard worker. Ask Mr. Crabtree."

Peer shook his head. "It's not going to happen."

He got into the car and closed the door behind him. I watched him through the open window. Suddenly I was mad. I had hung around the sessions, watching and listening and working, and he had barely noticed.

"The Wizard of Oz," I said.

"Beg your pardon?"

"You know, the man in the book. Dorothy and her friends asked him for what they wanted—brains, courage, a heart. But when they pulled back the curtain, he wasn't a wizard at all. He was a phony."

Peer started the engine and looked up at me. "Stay home and help your mother. She needs you. I don't."

He signaled to the others, and they drove off. I saw my future disappear with those two cars.

The world had changed and then moved on, out of town and out of reach. People had sung; the lathe had turned; *Popular Mechanics* had come alive. Science had gripped me, and music had shaken me, the way Daddy did when he was healing. Squeezing their heads. Grabbing their collars. Rolling them like dice. I'd seen them stumble back like they had been shoved.

Someone touched my shoulder. I turned and saw Sue Dean.

"What are you doing here?" I asked.

"Working. I just finished when Mr. Peer drove up. I saw what happened."

"I'm so stupid," I said.

"For getting mad at him?"

"For hoping. For dreaming."

"He's the one who's stupid," she said. "You really could have helped him."

"Camden, New Jersey. I wonder what it's like."

She smiled hopefully. "Bristol's a pretty nice place."

I shook my head. I shivered, even though it was the middle of summer. "I have to get out. I'm not staying in that tent. I can't breathe."

Sue Dean studied my face like she was trying to make a decision.

Finally she said, "There's something I want to show you."

PART III

WILDWOOD FLOWER

I'll sing, and I'll dance,
My laugh shall be gay,
I'll cease this wild weeping
Drive sorrow away

—A. P. Carter, "Wildwood Flower"

CHAPTER 17

We stood in a forest, surrounded by trees. A shaft of sunlight broke through, and Sue Dean's red hair blazed.

Leaning over, she showed me the faint outlines of a concrete step that was covered by dirt. Nearby, peeking out from some ferns, was another step and another. We followed them to a little clearing where a cabin was tucked out of sight.

The cabin was tiny, and it looked as old as the trees. The wood, though weathered, appeared sturdy enough. Sue Dean unlatched the door, and it swung open with a groan. I stepped inside.

There was one all-purpose room with a table, chairs, and a bed, beside which was a shelf with books on it. There was a lantern on the table and a woodstove in the corner, with logs stacked up next to it and an axe leaning against the wall. On the windows were flowered curtains, pulled back to let the sun in.

"What is it?" I asked.

"A special place. You're not the only one who has to get away, you know."

"Is it yours?"

"I think so," she said. "I was walking in the woods a few months ago and tripped on those steps. When I followed them, I found the cabin. I knocked on the door, but no one answered, so I came inside. The place was covered with dust. There was a book on the table, published in 1896."

"That was over thirty years ago. You think the cabin's that old?"

"It could be. Maybe it was used by moonshiners. Maybe a logger built it, then died before he could show anyone. Whatever happened, I was the first person who'd been here in a long time."

"Do your parents know?" I asked.

She shook her head. "I never showed anybody until today. I come here to get away from an ugly world. Maybe you could too."

I looked around. "It's old. But it's nice."

"I cleaned it up. I hung some curtains. I was here once in a big rainstorm, and it didn't leak. I think it's well built."

"I like it," I said.

Ralph Peer had left on Saturday, and the next morning Daddy had told me I wasn't grounded anymore. I was still a sinner, but I guess he figured there was less temptation.

I checked with Sue Dean, and that afternoon we rode our bikes down Virginia Avenue, which turned into Highway 421 south of town. We passed a sign for Crystal Caverns, which told me how she had known about it that day with Peer, and we headed for the mountains. They loomed over Bristol and included my favorite, Holston Mountain, a four-thousand-foot ridge with trails and streams. When you climbed it, you could look back at Bristol and see how small it was— just a smudge on the land. I'd made it that far a few times. Whatever Daddy felt about his tent, I thought God probably lived on that mountain, enjoying the breeze, taking in the view, watching hawks dive for food.

A few miles farther on, we entered Cherokee National Forest, where Sue Dean pulled off the road. We parked our bikes and headed up the trail surrounded by trees. There were sugar maples, yellow birch, beech trees. Trees had built Bristol. Lumber ran the town, along with things made from it—paper, boxes, furniture. But God only made so many trees, and there were fewer than there used to be. Across the canyon I could see hillsides that had been stripped bare, leaving rusted machinery, overgrown logging roads, and rotting stumps. They told the story of a lumber mill that was struggling.

Soon we were picking our way among the trillium, stands of white, three-petal flowers found in our part of the world. I stopped to study one and, after weeks of reading *Popular Mechanics*, thought it looked like an airplane propeller. Twenty minutes later we were inside the cabin.

Sue Dean pulled a box of cookies from a cabinet, and we sat down at the table. I took a fig newton and looked at it.

"I know what a fig is. What's a newton?"

She clonked me on the head with her knuckles. "It's what you get when you think too much."

It should have hurt, but it didn't bother me. In fact, I sort of enjoyed it. It seemed like the kind of thing Sister might have done if she were still around. Sometimes I imagined what it would have been like to have a girl in our house. Sister wasn't a ghost the way Daddy seemed to think. She had been real. We could have been friends.

"So, you like this place?" Sue Dean asked.

"It's private," I said.

She nodded. "It's special. It was mine. Now it's yours too."

Sue Dean closed her eyes like she was having a beautiful dream. She hummed and started to sing. It reminded me of Mama that night when she sang in the kitchen. But Sue Dean wasn't embarrassed. She seemed happy. Her voice started out raw and scratchy, then smoothed out. It blew across the room, reminding me of wind blowing through the trees.

I recognized "Amazing Grace," a song so famous that even I knew it. The words described a sinner, a wretch, maybe not very different from me. Then he got something called grace, which was like forgiveness but kept on going. I thought I could keep on going at that table, in that cabin, maybe for ten thousand years, like the song said.

That summer, Sue Dean and I rode to the cabin whenever we could. Once school started, it was hard getting there during the week, but we tried to go on Sundays. I brought a stack of *Popular Mechanics*, and Sue Dean supplied the food, leftovers she had sneaked from work. We would read or talk or just sit, listening to the birds. Sue Dean would sing. Sometimes it was Mama's song, or at least what I knew of it.

> Lord of the mountain
> Father on high
> Bend down and bless me
> Please won't you try

Listening to Sue Dean, I decided Mama's song was kind of like "Amazing Grace," except the grace was being asked for, not granted. I liked to think that God, if there was one, would bend down to help.

Mama struggled. So did I. I guess Daddy did too, but it was different for him because he thought he knew the answer, and he shared it every Saturday night. If you asked me though, the answer wasn't in what was shared. It was in the secrets, and the secrets were in that song.

CHAPTER 18

Sue Dean didn't like Gray, but my feelings about him weren't so simple. He was rich and liked to show it, but he was also sad. Sometimes I had the feeling that underneath it all was a nice person trying to get out. Then he would open his mouth, and I'd just shake my head.

Whatever I thought about Gray, I found myself going back again and again to his house, drawn by the gadgets and the Packard and the feeling that, on that hill, I could be whoever I wanted to be.

One day, when I was looking through a new stack of *Popular Mechanics* from Gray's house, I came across an article: "A Crystal Set for the Boy Builder" by Will H. Bates.

A crystal set, the article explained, was a homemade radio made up of a wooden base, some wire wrapped tightly in a coil, an antenna, a pair of earphones, and a "crystal holder," which was a small piece of crystal rock. Unlike most radios, a crystal set didn't need electrical power. Its power came from radio waves picked up by the antenna. The article, through instructions and diagrams, showed how to build a crystal set for less than four dollars.

I looked up from the magazine and gazed out the window. I saw a way into the future with that radio, like steps to the cabin. I went to my dresser and counted out some of the money I'd made doing chores for church members. I had plans for it.

***

Bunting's Drug Store on State Street sold a little bit of everything, and with the help of a store employee, I rounded up all the parts I needed to build the homemade radio called a crystal set. I carried them to the cash register, where the clerk stood watching me.

"What are these for?" she asked, smiling in a way that didn't seem too friendly. "Is your daddy cooking up something for that church of his? Electric communion cups? Spring-loaded pews?"

She glanced at the other employee, and he came down with a fit of coughing.

"No, ma'am," I said. "Just a few things for the house."

She bagged them up, and I left the store. Heading home, I remembered the way the clerk had looked at me. She thought Daddy was some kind of fool, and she lumped me in with him. I wondered how many other people in town felt that way.

For the rest of the week, I grabbed time whenever I could to work on the crystal set. I would lock my bedroom door and follow the directions in the magazine. By the end of the week my project was almost done.

On Sunday morning, Arnie and I helped Daddy clean up the church. Then Daddy and Mama went for a walk. As soon as they left, I ditched Arnie, grabbed the box where I kept my project, and pedaled off to the mountains. I was supposed to meet Sue Dean at the cabin, and I wanted to get ready.

There was no fog that day, so I could see Holston Mountain in the distance against the sky. I left my bike at the trailhead and hiked up to the cabin, lugging the box. I plopped it down on the table and pulled out my project, along with the magazine article. Flattening the pages, I studied the diagrams.

A few minutes later, Sue Dean arrived. When she saw me, her face brightened.

"What's this?" she asked.

"A surprise. Here, sit down."

The magazine was open on the table, and the nearly built crystal set was next to it. There was a wooden board that I'd sawed and sanded. Metal pins and holders were fastened to the board, with copper wire stretched between. At one end was a Quaker Oats canister that I'd turned on its side, wrapped with wire to form a coil, attached to the crystal rock, and screwed onto the board.

Sue Dean watched as I checked a diagram, then attached the last few parts, including a brass arm that ran at an angle from the board to the coil and could be swung across it.

I unwound the long antenna wire that the man at Bunting's

had found at the back of the store, and I connected it to the part of the set called the ground post. From there I looped the antenna around a pipe, ran it out the window, and hung the other end between two trees. Sue Dean followed me.

We came back inside, and I hooked up the final part of the crystal set: earphones. I put them on and said, "Here goes nothing."

I ran the brass arm across the coil. There was static in the earphones. I leaned in, listening more closely. Someone spoke, then there was music. It sounded like a fiddle. People were singing. Actual voices were coming through the air and into the cabin—beautiful voices.

"It works," I breathed. "It works!"

Sue Dean said, "Give me that."

Grabbing the earphones, she listened with one ear, her eyes open wide. She put the phones over both ears and pressed them against her head, like she was trying to squeeze out all the sound.

"It's science," I told her. "Science did that."

She closed her eyes and sang along, softly at first and then full-voiced, beaming. When the song ended, Sue Dean opened her eyes and handed back the earphones. I put them up to my ears and heard a man saying, "That was Dr. Humphrey Bate and His Possum Hunters. This is WSM, 'We Shield Millions,' broadcasting from the National Life and Insurance Company in Nashville, Tennessee."

Stunned, I took off the earphones and set them on the table.

"I built a radio," I said. "I have a place to play it."

"And someone to play it with," said Sue Dean.

We took turns with the earphones, then decided to listen at the same time, leaning our heads together and each using one earphone. Her face was close to mine. When she shut her eyes, I studied her up close. Her eyelashes were red and dusty. Her skin was like cream.

A little while later, we put down the earphones. I pulled out the fig newtons, and we went out on the front step to sit down.

"Where did you learn to sing like that?" I asked.

"Nowhere special." She glanced at me warily. "Mama says it's frivolous. Your daddy says it's a sin."

"It's beautiful," I said.

"You're crazy," she answered, but I noticed she was smiling.

We went back inside to the crystal set, leaning close to share the earphones. WSM was the strongest station, but there were others too—WWNC in Asheville, a naval station in Arlington, and, at the far end of the coil, WFBC in Knoxville, broadcasting from the First Baptist Church.

As we listened, I reached for the set at the same time she did, and our fingers bumped together. She gave my hand a squeeze, then smiled, closed her eyes, and sang along. Her rough, lovely voice filled the cabin, the way Mama's voice had filled the kitchen that night.

After a while she leaned back. "Oh, I almost forgot. Look what I found outside."

She reached into the pocket of her dress and pulled something out. Holding her palm flat, she showed me. It was a flower with six pointed petals, orange at the center and red on the tips.

"It's a lily," she told me. "Mama calls it a wildwood flower. She says it's kind of like of me, I guess because of the color. You can have it if you want."

She handed me the flower. I held it up in the sunlight and watched it shine.

CHAPTER 19

My family didn't know about Sue Dean. Then one Saturday night after church, she came marching up the aisle to where I stood with Mama and Arnie, waiting for Daddy to finish greeting people.

"Hey," she said, looking at me defiantly.

I glanced at Mama, who was staring at her.

Arnie asked, "Who are you?"

Instead of answering, Sue Dean poked me with her elbow.

"Uh, this is a friend of mine, Sue Dean Baker."

"She's a girl," said Arnie.

Sue Dean held out her hand to Mama. "Pleased to meet you, ma'am."

Mama shook her hand. "I'm Etta May Owens. You two know each other?"

"We met in town a few weeks ago," I said. "Her father works at the lumber mill."

"Where's your mother?" asked Mama.

"She's talking with some friends out front. I thought I'd come and say hi."

Arnie sang out, "Nate's got a girlfriend, Nate's got a girlfriend."

I reached for him, but he danced away.

Mama shot us a look. "In case you boys have forgotten, we're still in church." She and Sue Dean exchanged glances, and I could have sworn Mama rolled her eyes.

Sue Dean smiled. "I'd better go. Nice meeting you, Mrs. Owens."

"Same," said Mama.

Arnie watched her walk back up the aisle and out the entrance. Then he looked at me.

"Shut up," I said.

***

I heard that radio signals travel better at night and decided to find out if it was true. It would mean sneaking out after bedtime, but I thought I could do it. It would have to be on a Friday night, so there would be no school the next day.

When I told Sue Dean my plan, she looked me in the eye. "I'm going too."

I had learned a few things about Sue Dean since we had met. When she asked you something, she wanted an answer. When she told you something, she didn't.

I shrugged. "Okay."

A couple of weeks later, there was a Friday night with a full moon. I figured we'd need it to light the way. I waited until Mama and Daddy had gone to bed, then slipped out the window, got my bike, and walked it to the road, where I started to ride.

Sue Dean joined me a few blocks later, and we pedaled silently out of town, like a couple of explorers. The night was warm, and the moon had risen above the trees. Next to us, moon shadows skimmed along the ground, dark, flat versions of Sue Dean and me. Sue Dean herself looked different in the moonlight—pale, serious, thoughtful.

We reached the cabin after eleven, a time when I was usually fast asleep. It was strange to think that the world went on while I slept. Owls hooted. Cicadas sang. The earth moved through space, a tiny rock at the edge of the galaxy. On that rock, two specks came to a stop so close together it looked like they were touching.

I opened the door. It creaked in the darkness. Sue Dean lit the lantern. The crystal set glittered like gold.

What I had heard was true. The radio stations did come in better at night, with less static. Nashville was nearby, just outside the window. Sue Dean sang, and I listened. Along about midnight, we set down the earphones.

"I sure like this place," said Sue Dean. "I wish we could just stay here."

I looked around. The room flickered in the light of the lantern.

"I was surprised when you came up after the service," I said.

"I wanted to see what your family looked like."

"I'm glad."

"I like your mother. I don't know about your brother."

"He's an idiot," I said.

I thought about that night and all the nights at church. Daddy would preach, and my mind would struggle to escape.

I asked Sue Dean, "If you could start your own church, what would it be like?"

"You're funny," she said. "You can't wait to get out of church, but you want to start a new one."

"My church wouldn't have a cross. It would have a radio."

She smiled. "I'd like that."

"People wouldn't yell and jump around. They would just sit and listen. They would think."

"About what?"

"Science. Ideas. Why things are like they are."

"I'd come to your church," she said.

"What would you think about?"

She gazed down at her hands. They had bumps and calluses. They were strong, I could tell. "I'd think about Mama and Daddy. The way they work. The way they want things and can't have them."

Whatever Sue Dean was looking for, it probably was different from what her parents wanted. I thought of science class and the big diagram on the wall, showing the bones, muscles, and nerves in the human body. Watching Sue Dean,

I wondered if you could ever really know what was under a person's skin.

I leaned across the table, over the crystal set and earphones. She leaned too. We met in the middle, and our lips touched. There was a shock, like you get from a rug on a dry winter day, and we burst out laughing. Then we leaned in again and kissed. My fingers searched for hers and found them.

A moment later, we sat back. Sue Dean looked at me.

"You know what?" she said. "I think you have your church. I think this is it."

CHAPTER 20

And that's the way it was, through the fall and into the winter. Sue Dean and I would see each other at school, but our favorite times were at the cabin. Then December came, and the roads were covered with snow and ice, making our bike trips long, difficult, and sometimes dangerous. As a result, we didn't make it to the cabin very often and never at night. When we did, though, we found that the cabin walls kept the wind out, and the woodstove worked just fine. We used the axe to chop wood to feed the stove.

The sun came out a few days before Christmas and melted the snow, so we were able to steal an afternoon at the cabin to exchange gifts. I had bought Sue Dean some mittens, and she had knitted me a scarf. A month later we had our birthdays, both in January. So I bought her a scarf and she knitted me some mittens. We were fourteen years old. Our lives were all about getting away, which we did every chance we got.

Looking back, it's surprising that our families didn't find out. I guess they had more pressing things to think about. Sue Dean's parents were worried about work, money, and food.

Daddy and Arnie were worried about the everlasting God. Mama was worried about Daddy and Arnie.

Another reason they didn't find out was that I may have stretched the truth every now and then. I had told Mama and Daddy about Gray, and they didn't mind my going to visit him. I suppose it didn't hurt that his father was rich. So if I needed an excuse to sneak off to the cabin, I'd tell them I was going to Gray's house.

Meanwhile, the deeper we got into winter, the smaller the crowds got at church. Maybe it was the tent, which was hard to heat because of its size. Daddy bought some wood-stoves and set them out around the place, and Mr. Fowler donated a big coal-fired heater. Daddy called it his "hellfire machine," and I had to smile when folks clustered around it. Personally, I would have welcomed Satan himself if he'd been able to warm up that tent.

As the crowds dwindled, so did the money in the offering plate. I saw the plate go by every Saturday night, and it started looking pretty empty. Daddy said there was nothing as sad as a light offering plate. He tried to prime the pump, which meant putting some of his own money in there to start with. Sometimes when the plate reached the back of the tent, Daddy's dollar bills would be the only thing in it.

Daddy tried to preach the crowds back up. He got louder and holier. He got so holy his face would turn red, and there were nights when I thought his head would explode—just fly apart and scatter, half to heaven and half to hell, where the devil would see his holiness and laugh.

I would sit there, picturing comeuppance for Daddy or imagining myself at the cabin with Sue Dean. Arnie would perch beside me, back straight, eyes blinking, energy just pouring out of him, like God's battery. Mama would glance from Arnie to Daddy and back again, clenching her handkerchief and dabbing her cheeks. She tended to cry during services. I knew she wasn't crying about Daddy's message though. It was something else, something buried deep inside her, and it leaked out when Daddy was preaching.

Daddy was convinced that preaching would bring the crowds back, but I knew otherwise. Attendance was down because the town was down. People weren't buying tables and chairs and houses and whatever else you make out of wood, so the lumber mill was hurting, and workers were losing their jobs.

Finally, one day, Mama pulled me aside. "Things are getting bad for us, Nate. You know that, right?"

"You mean money?"

She nodded. "I don't know if you've noticed, but lately we've been eating a lot of beans. We've cut back all we can. We had a little nest egg, but it's gone."

"What does Daddy say?"

"You know him. He's off in heaven, jawing with Jesus. Arnie too. You and me, our feet are on the ground."

I'd never heard Mama talk that way about Daddy. I had figured whatever was fine with him was fine with her. I remembered the time she had dragged us to see Billy Sunday and get Daddy healed. Maybe Daddy wasn't the family leader at all. Maybe it was Mama. The thought was startling.

"What should we do?" I asked.

"I'll try to sell some of my sewing. You could get a job."

"A job? Really?"

"You're fourteen years old, Nate. When I was your age, some of my friends were already working."

"I suppose I could get a job after school. But what?"

She gazed at me. Suddenly it was obvious.

"Mr. Lane," I said.

"You already help with his car. Maybe he'd pay you."

The next day I mentioned the idea to Mr. Lane. He clapped me on the shoulder, and, for one of the only times I could remember, he actually grinned.

"Splendid!" he said. "You can start today."

That was a Saturday, and by the following week he had set up a schedule for me. Two days each week, I would wash the car and work on it when he got home. I'd wax it on Saturdays and fix anything that went wrong. But that wasn't the best part.

"He's letting you drive?" exclaimed Gray when I told him. "What about me?"

I shrugged. "You should ask him."

"I did. He said no."

Seeing that he felt bad, I told him, "It's not for fun. It's for work. I need to drive it if I'm going to fix it."

There was talk of passing a law that drivers would need a license, but in the meantime anyone could do it, which was fine with me and apparently with Mr. Lane. The next Saturday after I waxed the car, he asked me to drive him and Gray into town to run some errands. I pulled out from their driveway onto Taylor Street, taking it slow.

"What do you think?" asked Mr. Lane.

"It's beautiful," I breathed.

We drifted past the mansions on Maryland Avenue and Poplar Street. It was like a dream. Under the hood, things were firing and turning and pumping up and down, but inside the car, it was as quiet as the Lanes' front hall.

As for me, I felt like I'd been driving my whole life, like settling into those soft leather seats, I was finally where I belonged. It wasn't about engines or car repairs or nuts and bolts—it was a feeling. It just seemed right.

Turning onto State Street, I drove under the Bristol sign and past the hat company. Mr. Lane asked me to pull up in front of Bunting's Drug Store, and when we did, I saw Sue Dean. Or rather, she saw me. I gave her a wave and a sheepish smile. She stared, then turned away.

When I saw her at school the next day, she glared at me. "Nate, what are you doing?"

"I have a job."

"You work for him?"

I didn't know whether to be proud or embarrassed. "Mr. Lane hired me. I'm part mechanic, part driver. Part grunt."

"He's a terrible person," she said.

"We need the money, like your father does. Like you do."

"What about his son? Trey or whatever. Are you really his best friend?"

"Maybe I'm his best friend, but he's not mine. And his name is Gray."

"That's not a name. It's a paint color."

"Look, I admit Mr. Lane isn't the greatest person, but he gave me a job."

"He's firing everybody else."

"It's not just his fault, you know. The mill isn't selling lumber. They have to cut back."

"Are you his publicist? What did Mr. Peer call it—his agent?"

Hearing that name took me back—to the hat company, to the sessions, to the music and the hope that it might set me free. Only it hadn't. I was stuck in Bristol with a crazy family, working for a terrible man, pretending to like his son, and arguing with Sue Dean, my real best friend.

CHAPTER 21

Sue Dean and I patched up our differences, but the damage was done. Winter had come. Dark clouds descended. The cold settled in.

At the cabin, things were strained. At school, my grades were dropping because of the job. At home, we never had enough money. I gave Mama my checks from Mr. Lane, but it was like dropping them down a deep hole.

I had trouble sleeping, and sometimes late at night I'd hear Mama and Daddy talking. I couldn't hear the words, just the tone of their voices, but I could tell they were scared. The next Saturday night, Daddy's preaching would be louder and more desperate. The swampy pit of sin got bigger each week.

"Beware!" he would bellow. "We're sinking!"

The people would shout and jump and make sounds I'd never heard outside the tent. I'd squirm and sink lower in my seat. Daddy would rail against dirt, gluttony, xylophones, and science. Then he would get to subject of music, and he'd glare down at me.

One night I got fed up and glared back. Hard. He hesitated, then stopped and seemed to make a decision.

He asked the crowd, "Have you all met my son? Not Arnie, my little firecracker. I'm talking about his big brother, Nate. Come up here, Nate."

I didn't move. I wasn't part of his show.

Arnie shot me a crazy grin and started chanting, "Nate! Nate! Nate! Nate!"

The crowd joined in. The place rocked.

Next to me, Mama whispered, "Oh, for Pete's sake, go on up there. It won't kill you."

I did it for Mama, not for Daddy. Never for Daddy.

Rising, I began walking to the front. His gaze was fastened on me, like a rope pulling me in. When I reached him, he grabbed my shoulders and turned me around to face the crowd.

"He has the bug," said Daddy. "He has the cancer. Music! Music!" Daddy squeezed my head in his hands and started to pray. "Jesus, help him. Clear his ears and his thoughts. Purify this, your sinful son. Drive out those evil notes."

I struggled, then stopped. I heard a melody, not from the radio like before. This one was inside me. It was Mama's song, gentle and pure. As Daddy prayed, it grew until it filled me. It was a feeling, like you get on Christmas morning. There were gifts to be opened, secrets to be discovered. There was truth, and I would find it.

Daddy didn't know it, but as he pronounced his hateful words, he was praying me out of the tent, out of his grip, and into the sweet, sad arms of music.

***

Winter turned to spring, and the offering plate got emptier. I spent more time helping Mr. Lane, trying to earn extra money. I fixed the Packard and drove him around town, sometimes with Gray but mostly without.

I came to realize that my friendship wasn't with Gray, or even with Mr. Lane. It was with the car. When I opened the hood and listened to the hum of the engine, I was in a world that worked, a world that made sense.

One Sunday, Sue Dean was busy, so we couldn't go to the cabin. Daddy and Arnie went into town, and I spent some time in the cemetery. I was by myself there, but I felt like I had company. There were people all around me, their bodies in Bristol and their souls elsewhere. Kind of like me.

As I crossed the street and went back into the house, I started to call out but then heard something. It was Mama, singing her song. The door to Mama and Daddy's room was open a crack, so I crept down the hall and peered inside. Mama sat on the bed, humming softly, with a shoebox in her lap. She was going through some things in the box, but I couldn't make out what they were. After a few minutes she stopped, sighed, and closed the box. Moving to the closet, she placed it on the top shelf, then shut the closet door and turned back in my direction.

I ducked out of the way and sneaked off to the kitchen, where I went outside and came back in with a slam of the screen door.

"Hello," I called.

She entered the kitchen, and I noticed that her cheeks were wet.

"Hi, sweetheart," she said.

"Are you okay?" I asked.

She wiped her cheeks and cupped my face in her hands. "I'm fine."

Later that day, when I had the house to myself, I went to Mama and Daddy's room. Opening the closet, I got the shoebox down from the shelf. I knew the box was private, and I wasn't supposed to be in their room, but I couldn't help myself. I sat on the bed, opened the lid, and looked inside.

It was Sister's box.

You have to understand, at my house, Sister was more of a ghost than a person. Daddy talked about her. He talked *to* her and would get pretty worked up. Then he'd listen for an answer, and sometimes he heard one, like the time she helped name his church.

Sister had died when I was two, so I barely remembered her. Besides Daddy's rantings, the main way I knew about her was from a photograph on the mantel, taken a few months before she passed. It showed all four of us, when I was two and Sister was six. We looked happy, which was amazing in light of what was to come. As far as I knew, that was the one photo we had of Sister. Until now.

The box was filled with Sister things—baby shoes, ribbons, a lock of hair, a drawing made with crayons. And there was a stack of photos showing her at church, in the yard, in the kitchen wearing an oversized apron and gripping a wooden spoon. In that picture her mouth was smeared with something—pancake batter, I guess—and her smile filled the room.

Next to the stack was a slip of paper. I unfolded it and saw Mama's writing. She had used a pencil to write the first few lines of her song. There was sadness in those words, and wishing. It was like a prayer, not Daddy's kind but the real kind.

At the bottom of the box, smudged like it had been handled over and over again, was one last photo. It was a picture of a gravestone with just a few words on it.

Sweet Sister
1910–1916

I imagined Mama touching the photo, running her fingers over it and humming her song. I recalled the story Mama told, of Daddy hugging that grave in the rain, trying to climb in, and Mama dragging him off to see Billy Sunday and get healed. Somehow it all went together, but I didn't understand how.

I stayed there for a long time, thinking about Sister, trying to remember her. Then I closed the box, put it back on the shelf, and shut the closet door.

CHAPTER 22

By the time summer came, Bristol was hurting, and it showed. Families roamed the streets, begging for food—people we knew, hardworking people I'd seen at church and school. I wanted to help them but didn't know how. Besides, we weren't doing so well ourselves.

Daddy always said when you give to the church, it should be your first dollar. But it seemed that some of the people disagreed. The first dollar went for food, the second for clothes, the third for shelter, and sometimes that's all there was.

"We need a jolt," Daddy said after breakfast one Saturday morning. He had just come out of what he called a prayer consultation, something he did before church services to check in with Jesus and plan the service accordingly.

"A jolt?" I said. "Does God use electricity?"

Recently I had stopped thinking my comments and started saying them. Daddy didn't much like it.

"Not an electric jolt," he snapped. "A spirit jolt, a faith jolt. A Jesus jolt."

"Oh Lord," said Mama, who stood nearby washing the dishes. The tougher things got, the harder she scrubbed. I noticed that Mama had started saying comments too, but Daddy didn't seem to notice hers. Most of them just bounced off.

Mama handed a dripping plate to Arnie, who was drying. He recently had turned nine and was still Daddy's biggest fan. He even asked if he could preach, but Daddy said no. I shivered at the thought.

When I went to the tent that night, I was surprised to see Sue Dean standing at the entrance.

"Hey," she said. "You have a minute?"

"Are you coming to the service?" I asked.

"Not this time. I wanted to talk."

Mama stood nearby, waiting for me. I heard Daddy inside, starting to warm up the crowd.

"Can we do it later?" I asked her.

Sue Dean took a few strands of hair and twisted them, the way I'd seen her do when she was worried.

"I guess."

"Is something wrong?" I asked.

"I need to see you."

I realized we hadn't spoken in several days, and two weeks had passed since we'd been to the cabin.

"How about tonight, after the service? At the cabin?"

"It's important," she said.

"Nine o'clock. I'll be there. I promise."

She gazed into my eyes, then nodded and left.

I joined Mama, and we went inside. "Where's Arnie?" I asked her.

"Fiddling around in his room. Said he'd be here directly."

The people filed in, and a few minutes later Daddy entered from behind the altar. He was wearing his good suit, the one with a cross on the pocket made out of sequins. He asked the people to take their seats, then spread out his arms.

"Folks, we've got us some trouble," he announced in that booming voice of his.

"Amen!" some people called back.

"I'm not talking about money trouble. That's the easy kind. We've got something worse—break-your-back, Lord-have-mercy, take-it-to-Jesus, spirit trouble."

"Preach it!" somebody yelled.

"I tried that," he answered, "but you folks wouldn't listen."

I glanced at Mama. She looked back, worried. Daddy preached fire and brimstone, but usually he didn't insult the congregation.

Daddy went on. "I tried shouting. I tried healing and laying on hands. I'm not too proud to tell you it didn't work. The spirit sagged. It sputtered like wet fireworks. So tonight, I'm bringing out the heavy artillery."

He stepped behind the altar and came back holding a big, boxy object that was covered with a blanket. The people around us didn't know what it was. But I did, and so did Mama.

"Jesus God," she breathed.

From the beginning, Mama had begged Daddy to get rid of the snake, but a year had passed and it hadn't happened. He kept it in that cage on a table in the shed, and he'd go stare at it. I knew for a fact that Arnie still went in there sometimes. He'd get a crazy look in his eye, then, I suppose, he repented.

Me, I had learned to live with it. After all, we'd been hearing for years that Satan was just around the corner. Now he was in the shed. Was that really so different?

Daddy still had plans for it. He'd told me a dozen times. When the time was right, he would take out that poisonous snake and handle it like a dang Chihuahua, cradling it in his arms, petting it, maybe even kissing it. If his faith was strong enough, the snake wouldn't hurt him. God would win. Simple as that.

I had hoped he would never actually try it, but apparently the day had arrived. He was ready. He looked up at the congregation. Heaven shone on his face.

"Behold," he declared, "Beelzebub!"

He whipped off the blanket. Under it was the cage. Only problem was, the cage was empty.

CHAPTER 23

"Beelzebub!" Daddy thundered. "He's gone!"

There was a low murmur at the back of the tent, and it grew louder. Someone screamed.

I looked back. Arnie was walking up the aisle like a bride on her wedding day. The snake coiled around his arm, up and over his shoulder. It rattled wildly and peered across the tent, its tongue flicking.

As for Arnie, he was blazing. I had no doubt that if I touched his cheek, I'd get burned. He grinned like a madman.

"No!" shrieked Mama.

She tried to push past me and reach him, but I held her back.

"Be careful," I told her. "Don't startle the snake."

The people had backed away, giving Arnie plenty of room, but Daddy had no such hesitation. He strode down the aisle, coat flapping as if in a holy wind. He and Arnie stopped and faced each other—tall and short, father and son, crazy and crazier.

Beelzebub hissed and rattled.

Daddy held out his hand. "Give him to me, Son."

"He's mine," said Arnie, with a little lilt in his voice.

Drops appeared on Daddy's brow, squeezed right out of his pores. "He's not yours or mine, Son. He belongs to Satan."

Arnie stuck out his chin. "I can handle him."

"I'm not so sure," said Daddy.

"I am," said Arnie.

Maybe they would have worked it out. We'll never know, because at that moment, right next to Arnie, a baby let out a holler. Beelzebub shook his head, I swear, the way I'd seen people do when they're startled by a loud noise.

Then he struck.

He bit Arnie's hand and latched on. Arnie shrieked and slumped to the ground. Daddy kneeled down, grabbed the snake, and yanked him off. Beelzebub slithered into the crowd.

There was a moment of silence as people realized what had happened. Then the place exploded. People jumped on their chairs or sprinted for the exits. It was a mob scene, right there in Daddy's church.

I once read in *Popular Mechanics* about a woman, just a tiny thing, who lifted a car off her child. They said she got her power from something called *adrenaline*. Maybe Mama had adrenaline, because suddenly there she was, picking up Arnie and draping him over her shoulder like a dish towel. She grabbed me by the arm, then raced down the aisle and out the back, with me stumbling along behind. She didn't stop until we were inside our house, where she slammed the door and locked it tight. I called the hospital, while she laid Arnie down on the couch.

A minute later Daddy pounded on the door. I let him in, and he hurried over to the couch. By that time Arnie was looking bad. His hand was puffed up, his skin was clammy white, and he said it felt like a red-hot sword was stabbing him. Every few minutes he would double up and vomit—on his shirt, on the couch, on Mama. She didn't care. She just knelt there next to him, stroking his forehead and praying.

"Will he be all right?" moaned Daddy.

"Shut up," said Mama.

After what seemed like a week, the ambulance got there, siren wailing. They loaded Arnie into the back, Mama climbed in with him, and they sped off into the darkness.

Daddy and I sat on the back step. I looked around, trying to figure out what had happened. The night seemed perfectly normal, but things had changed. Maybe Satan was real. Maybe he had killed Arnie.

That's when I remembered Sue Dean.

Glancing at my watch, I saw that it was past ten o'clock. I mumbled an excuse to Daddy, got on my bike, and pedaled to the trailhead. Slinging the bike aside, I ran up the trail. Soon I was at the cabin. I opened the door.

"Sue Dean?"

There was no answer. The cabin was empty. On the table was a note.

Dear Nate,

I was here at 9:00. I'm sorry you didn't come. I waited as long as I could, but then I had to go.

There was trouble at the lumber mill. The union had a meeting, and Mr. Lane found out. He told them to break it up, but they wouldn't. My father grabbed Mr. Lane and threatened him. Mr. Lane fired my father and called the police.

We have to leave town tonight. My father says we can't wait. I shouldn't have come to the cabin, but I wanted to say goodbye. It was important to me. I guess it wasn't important to you.

Maybe it's better this way. You're a friend of Grayson Lane. You might not want to be my friend too.

Sue Dean

Grabbing the note, I charged out of the cabin and down the trail, hopped on my bike, and pedaled furiously back to town. I had only been to Sue Dean's house once or twice, but I managed to find it. The place was empty. Looking around frantically, I saw the red tip of a burning cigarette on the porch next door. I hurried over and found an older man sitting on a porch swing, smoking and sipping iced tea.

"You're out late," he grunted.

"Yes, sir. Do you know what happened to the Bakers? I'm a friend of Sue Dean's."

"Sure do. I was there. We were having a union meeting at the mill, and Lane showed up with his goons. He yelled at us, and Baker grabbed him. Lane fired him on the spot. Baker came back to his family, and they packed up."

"Do you know where they went?" I asked.

The man shook his head. "Away."

"You suppose they went home? They were from Virginia."

"I don't think so. He said they would try someplace new."

"Where?"

"He didn't tell us, and we didn't ask." The man glanced around nervously. "Sometimes it's better not to know."

Sue Dean had been worried. She had tried to tell me, but I hadn't listened. She had waited for me, and I hadn't come.

And now she was gone.

CHAPTER 24

As it turned out, Arnie survived, thanks to Mama and the doctors. His arm swelled up to twice its normal size, and he had terrible pain, but the doctors had stored some antivenom for just such a case. They shot him full of it, and a few days later he was feeling better. His symptoms hung on, and he was constantly going back to the doctor, but he was alive.

I couldn't say the same for Daddy's church. We searched for Beelzebub the next day but didn't find him. A rumor started that he lived under the tent and came out when people prayed, which didn't do much for attendance.

Daddy was subdued but didn't want to give up. On Wednesday night almost no one was at the service. By Saturday night it was just him preaching and Mr. Fowler barking. Daddy tried a few more times, but there was no getting around it. The church was dead, with no resurrection in sight.

Not long after that, Daddy closed up shop and sold the tent. I saw it a few times out on Highway 11, part of a flea market they held on Sunday afternoons. Mama thought it was sad, but I didn't. Daddy always said you reap what you sow, and that's what had happened. His religion wasn't real. It was made up, a rickety thing he had pieced together, like trying to build a car from old tractor parts.

Truth be told, I'm not sure Daddy's church would have lasted, with or without Beelzebub. If you stick your finger in an electrical socket, you jump around for a while. Pretty soon, though, it wears off. You stop jumping. Maybe you sit down to rest and recover. Daddy brought people to a fever pitch, but they didn't stay that way for long. They couldn't live like that. No one can.

With church gone, Daddy spent a lot of time brooding about what he had done to Arnie and about Sister. Daddy's church had taken his mind off Sister for a while, but with the church gone, she was back. Daddy prayed about her. I know because I heard him—at the table, on the porch, in the shed. Sometimes he mumbled and sometimes he shouted. We tried to ignore it, but I could feel him pulling us down to the dark place where he lived.

I had a dark place of my own. Sue Dean was there. She never had asked much of me, and when she did, I had let her down. I thought of our times at the cabin and how we had listened to music together. I didn't go there now. The cabin had been our special place, and it wouldn't be right to go there by myself. Staying away was like a punishment for what I'd done.

The crystal set, the books, the flowered curtains, the stack of *Popular Mechanics*—I left them all there. Maybe someone else would stumble across the cabin, see them, and wonder who had been there.

Meanwhile I was trapped inside Daddy's house, and I could barely stand it. The days dragged. The nights pressed down. I'd lie in bed, imagining a better place. Sometimes I'd go to the window, look up at Holston Mountain, and think of that night with Sue Dean, when we rode our bikes and escaped together.

After the church closed, Daddy needed to earn some money, and he'd never been very good at it. He picked up a few odd jobs, but most people turned him away. I guess if somebody saves your immortal soul, you feel funny hiring him to wash your windows.

With school out, I put in more hours working for Mr. Lane, partly to help with money and partly because it was the one thing left that I enjoyed. I knew every inch of the Packard, and somehow that made driving it seem better. But I paid a price. I would haul Mr. Lane around town, and sometimes I'd imagine Sue Dean standing on the curb, glaring at us as we passed.

Every Friday afternoon Mr. Lane went to the Bristol Bank on State Street, and one week Gray came along, sitting in the back seat with his father to make sure everyone knew I worked for them. When we got to the bank, a crowd was waiting for us, yelling and shaking their fists. I recognized the man who had lived next door to the Bakers. I waved, and he scowled.

As we pulled up, the crowd surrounded the car, shouting.

"Up with the union!"

"Lane, go home!"

"We need jobs!"

I saw people who had come to Daddy's church, decent people who were desperate. They pushed up against the car. Behind me, Gray shrank back, gripping his father's arm.

For some reason I wasn't scared. I was angry, like the people. They were losing their jobs, fired by a man who drove a Packard and lived in a mansion on the hill. Suddenly I wondered what I was doing in that car.

Mr. Lane sat behind me, calm and cold, his stiff expression like a coat of armor. He gave a nod, and a police whistle sounded. Four uniformed officers appeared, holding billy clubs.

"That's enough!" they yelled. "Get out of here!"

The protesters pulled back. They gave a few more shouts, then broke up and headed off.

One of the officers approached the car. "Sorry, sir."

He walked Mr. Lane into the bank. Gray shot me a grin. "We showed them."

"We?" I said.

"You and me. Dad. Us."

Hearing his words, thinking about what they meant—something inside me burst. "I'm not us. I'm not you."

"Huh?"

"I'm the hired help. I'm not us. I'm them. Those people."

Gray stared at me. "No, you're not."

"You think we're friends? How come you've never been to my house? Why haven't you asked about my family? You've never even met them."

"Your father's a preacher. I know that."

"The church closed," I told him. "Now he's doing odd jobs for people like you."

"You have a brother, don't you?"

"His name is Arnie. A few weeks ago he almost died."

"I'm sorry," Gray mumbled.

"But you know all the important stuff, like your latest gadgets."

"You like my gadgets," he said.

Mr. Lane was back in a minute, his pants creased, his shirt starched, every hair in place. You'd never know he had just faced an angry crowd. How did he escape without a smudge? The answer had been in the police officer's face and in the easy way Mr. Lane carried himself.

Power.

It's what I wanted, what I didn't have, what had run Sue Dean out of Bristol.

I hated it.

Mr. Lane stood beside the car, brushing dust from his suit.

"Do you remember a man named Harley Baker?" I asked him.

"Baker. Hmm, yes. Union."

"You had a fight with him."

Mr. Lane snorted. "That wasn't a fight. I fired him."

"Like all the others," I said.

He shot me a little smile. "It's simple economics."

I wanted to wipe that smile off his face. I wondered if Sue Dean's father had felt the same way when he had grabbed Mr. Lane.

"You're hurting people," I told him. "You're ruining lives."

"Just doing my job," he said. But I noticed that he wasn't smiling anymore.

"You don't just fire them. You beat them up. You make them bleed. Or at least your goons do."

"Goons?" he said.

"That's what the union calls them. But you know that."

He gazed at me. "Why are we talking about this?"

"Because it's wrong," I said.

"Let's go home," said Gray from the back seat.

I had to say something more, to speak up for Sue Dean and her father, and maybe most of all for myself. The words tumbled out.

"Mr. Lane," I said, "you're a terrible person."

It was out there, and I couldn't bring it back. I didn't want to.

His eyes narrowed. The gaze turned into a glare. Something in his face slammed shut.

"Get out of the car," he said.

With those words, he cut me out of his life, the way he'd cut out all the workers at the mill. In the end, I was just another employee, and employees can be fired. Simple economics.

Gray looked at his father, confused. Without his gadgets, he was a small, sad boy.

I opened the door, got out, and shut it behind me. There was a satisfying *thunk*, a deep, solid sound that only a Packard makes. I ran my hand over the perfect green paint. Then I stepped back, and Mr. Lane got in. He pushed a button, and there was a low hum, the sound of a big engine running smoothly.

"You're a fool," he said. But when I looked at his face, I saw that he was sad too.

He adjusted the mirror and drove off down State Street. Gray, still in the back seat, watched me as they disappeared around the corner.

CHAPTER 25

Mama and Daddy heard about what had happened at the bank. It seemed that everybody in town did. At supper that night, sitting at the kitchen table, Daddy asked me about it.

"There were fifty people or so," I told him.

"Was there a fight?" asked Arnie, his eyes gleaming.

"The police broke it up," I said.

"What about you?" asked Mama, worried. "Are you all right?"

"Sort of."

Daddy looked at me funny.

"I wasn't hurt," I said. "No one was. But it made me mad, all those people that Mr. Lane fired. I told him so. That he was ruining their lives."

"You said that?" asked Daddy.

"Yes, because it's true."

"What did he do?"

I shrugged. "I guess you could say he fired me."

"Fired you!" It was Daddy's best Jesus voice, the one that roared and made people wince. But it didn't scare me.

"Yes, sir," I said.

"What's wrong with you?" he demanded. "We need that money!"

I thought of an expression I'd heard Sue Dean use. "It's blood money," I said. "He earned it by hurting people. I don't want it."

"I do!" said Daddy.

He was lit up. I needed to put out the flame.

"Then you earn it," I snapped. "You're the father. Get a job—a real one, not screeching at people and dancing with snakes."

He gaped at me.

Mama's face went white. "Apologize to your father," she said. "And to Arnie."

"He's the one who should apologize," I told her. "To you, to me, especially to Arnie. Our family's in trouble, all because of his phony religion."

"Phony!" said Daddy.

"It's not real. It's pieces and parts. You take what you want and throw away the rest—things like science and music."

At the sound of the word, Daddy got wild-eyed, almost scared. "Get thee behind me, Satan!"

"Music isn't evil," I told him. "It's good."

"Jesus, shut my ears!" said Arnie.

I gave Daddy a hard look, like the one Mr. Lane had given me. "Maybe there is no Satan. Or maybe it's you."

"Nathan!" exclaimed Mama. "Go to your room!"

I shoved back my chair and went into the hall, but I didn't go to my room. I went to theirs. I opened the closet, took out the shoebox, and carried it back to the kitchen.

When Mama saw it, she froze. Daddy stared.

"What's that?" asked Arnie.

"Our family has secrets," I told him. "They're in this box."

"Give it to me," said Mama in a choked-up voice.

I said, "I'm sorry, Mama. It's not just yours. It's ours too."

Daddy was twitching and shivering.

"This is Sister's box," I said. "It's filled with her things."

I opened the box and showed it to Arnie. He reached inside.

"Pictures," he said. "Where did these come from?"

Mama was crying. Daddy was making noises in his throat.

I took out the slip of paper and unfolded it. "There's words to a song: 'Lord of the mountain...'"

"No!" screamed Mama.

Daddy's face got red, like he was going to explode.

Arnie lifted out one of the photos. "What's this one?"

I took it from him and looked. "That's Sister's grave."

Daddy bellowed and then struck, like the snake. He leaped toward me, knocking over his chair, and grabbed my arm. I dropped the box, and the contents spilled across the floor—baby shoes, the lock of hair, photos.

Mama sank to the floor. On her hands and knees, she

tried to gather up her precious things, while Daddy and I struggled.

"A fight!" shrieked Arnie, eyes gleaming again, egging us on like some twisted cheerleader.

Daddy reached for the photo of Sister's grave, and I held it away from him. He let out an angry roar and backhanded me across the face, stunning me for a moment. Grabbing the photo, he pulled. I pulled back.

There was a ripping sound. We stopped and gaped. Sister's grave was torn in two—like me, like the whole stupid town of Bristol.

Slowly, deliberately, I put my half on the table. I reached up and touched the corner of my mouth. It was bleeding.

Daddy collapsed into a chair and leaned over the torn photo. Lining up the two halves, he stared sadly at Sister's final resting place. Arnie brought him some tape, and Daddy tried to put them back together.

I turned and walked off.

PART IV

THE WANDERING BOY

Out in the cold world and far away from home
Somebody's boy is wandering alone
No one to guide him and keep his footsteps right
Somebody's boy is homeless tonight

—A. P. Carter, "The Wandering Boy"

CHAPTER 26

The whistle blew. The freight train started to move.

We watched from behind some shrubs at the edge of the railroad yard. The steam engine rolled slowly toward us— huge, black, iron wheels taller than a man.

"Now?" I asked.

"Wait," he said.

The engine labored by, picking up speed.

"Now?" I asked.

"Not yet," he said.

The coal car followed, then a long, flat car loaded with lumber. Behind it came a boxcar. The door was open.

"Now!" he said.

He lit out from behind the shrubs, limping but moving with surprising speed. I followed, backpack bumping as I ran. When we reached the boxcar, he trotted alongside, then gripped one of the two metal bars beside the open door. Swinging sideways, he grabbed the other bar and pulled himself up and through the door.

Then it was just the train and me. The noise was

tremendous—clacking and whirring, groaning and rumbling, as much a feeling as a sound. One step and I was on my way. One slip and I'd go under.

I reached for one of the bars, closed my hand around it, and squeezed. Then, remembering the way he'd done it, I turned sideways and reached for the other bar. As I touched it, my foot hit a rock and I stumbled.

Suddenly I was dangling one-armed from the train.

I bumped the boxcar and bounced off. My feet dragged on the ground. My hand, damp with sweat, started to slip. The wheels clattered and roared, just inches away.

He grabbed my wrist. Others gripped my arm, collar, belt. I flew up and into the boxcar, skidding on my elbows and knees.

"Nice landing," he said.

His name was Bill, or at least that's what he had told me. Early that morning he had spotted me in the railroad yard, headed for one of the parked trains.

He had yanked me aside and said, "What do you think you're doing?"

Leaving home, I wanted to say. *Going away and never coming back.*

"Getting on the train," I told him.

He was a small, wiry man who could have been thirty or sixty. His face was grimy, and his tattered clothes hung loose. He walked with a limp.

"Don't get on here," he said, looking around the yard. "If the bulls see you, they'll beat you up, then take your money and whatever else you've got."

"Bulls?"

"Railroad police. They're thugs, hired to scare us off. Don't let 'em catch you."

"Then how do I get on?" I asked.

"Go to the edge of the yard. Wait till a train starts moving." He looked at me and sighed. "Come on, I'll show you."

An hour later I was in the boxcar. Bill and the others sat on the floor, leaning against the wall. There were three more besides him—a Negro man, a teenage boy, and a woman wearing jeans, a work shirt, and a look that said, *I'm tougher than you.*

I couldn't sit. I was too excited or scared, or maybe both. I shrugged off my backpack and set it next to Bill, then stepped over to the door and looked out. The town of Bristol rolled by. But this wasn't the pretty Bristol I was used to. It was the back side, the side facing the tracks.

There were clotheslines, trash dumps, abandoned cars. People worked and talked and yelled and fought. They showed you things you'd never see out front. A woman whipped a dog. A man stood at a washtub, shirt off, scrubbing under his arms. Children argued and played. A boy with dark skin and a missing tooth waved at us, and I waved back.

Soon Bristol was gone, replaced by hills and then mountains. It was summer, and the trees were full green. The sugar maples were my favorites. Beneath the trees were trillium and roses. I thought of the wildwood flower Sue Dean had given me, and I took it from my wallet, where I kept it pressed in waxed paper. The flower had dried and was falling apart, but I could still make out the color—orange in the center and red at the tips, like Sue Dean's hair.

The train labored up the mountain's grade. A hot breeze blew. Bristol was behind me. I didn't know what lay ahead. All I knew was I had to get out.

One by one, my reasons for staying had been taken away—Ralph Peer, Sue Dean, the job. Now the only thing left was my family, which was what I'd been trying to escape in the first place. Released from the tent, they were bearing down on me. The fight with Daddy had been the final push. It was time to go.

The morning after our fight, I got up before dawn and put a few things in my backpack. I reached into a drawer and pulled out a roll of bills held together by a rubber band. There wasn't much—maybe ten dollars I'd saved up—but it would have to do.

I found a pencil and scribbled a note. *I'm leaving. It's better this way.*

Taking the note, I tiptoed to the kitchen. Mama had left the shoebox on the counter from the night before, and inside was the taped-up photo of Sister's grave. I studied the photo, then slipped it into my wallet. I left the note next to the box, then walked out the door.

CHAPTER 27

Why do people ride the rails?

Some say it's the sights. If you're on a freight train, you see things you never noticed before—faces, factories, chimneys. Beyond them, the world stretches off in the distance, waiting to be discovered.

Some say it's the smells. One man claimed to love cinder and smoke. He wore them on his clothes like a badge. I didn't believe it though. The smells I remembered were stale urine, spoiled food, and people who needed a bath.

Some say it's the taste or touch. When you're hungry and alone, half a sandwich can seem like a feast. A pat on the shoulder lasts for days.

For me, it was the sounds—the click of the rails, the clang of a crossing, the shriek of the whistle going around the bend. It was music, train music. I heard it for the first time as I stood in the boxcar door that morning, watching the trees go by.

We traveled north and west into Virginia, across Clinch Mountain, through Hamilton Gap, over Big Moccasin Creek. Just the names got me excited. Bill recited them as they went by. He told me he was headed for a little town called Mendota, to find his wife.

"I left a year ago looking for work," he said. "That's why I was in Bristol. I went to the lumber mill, but they turned me away. It was the same most places. No jobs. I'd been planning to send money home to my wife, but recently when I've written to her, the letters have been returned and not opened."

"Where do you think she went?" I asked.

"That's what I aim to find out."

I thought of Mama, Daddy, and Arnie. "Do you have any children?"

"None, thank God." He caught himself. "No offense. How old are you?"

"Eighteen," I lied.

"It's hardest on the kids," he said. "I see them hopping freight trains—sixteen, fifteen, some no more than twelve. They've got no place to go, at home or on the road." He looked me over. "You're new to this. Riding the rails."

I nodded.

"Two pieces of advice," he said. "If there's something you can't afford to lose, put it in your shoes. Don't take it out. That's for emergencies. And if you walk on top of a train, always face the front, so you'll see what's coming. Otherwise the curves will catch you by surprise and throw you off. Oh, and one other thing. Don't let 'em call you a bum. You're a hobo."

I glanced around at the boxcar and the scenery flying by. "A hobo. Yeah, I guess that fits."

He grunted. "Welcome to the club."

I was riding the rails, part of a club I'd never thought about.

"Where you headed?" asked Bill.

"Anyplace."

"So it's like that."

"I could get off at Mendota," I said.

He shook his head. "The police there don't like strangers. But if you go a few more stops, you hit Gate City. I stopped there once. You could stay at the jungle."

I must have had a funny expression on my face, because he chuckled.

"That's what they call it," he told me. "It's a camp for hoboes. Head for the railroad yard, and turn right at the creek. You'll see it."

Suddenly I saw danger in Bill's eyes. He took my arm and hustled me to the back of the car, away from the door and into the shadows. The others were already there, huddled in a corner. We heard the clomp of work boots on the roof. A moment later someone climbed down the ladder, glanced inside, and then left.

We were quiet for a while longer, then Bill said in a soft voice, "That was a brakeman. They check, but not often and not very well. If you stay out of sight, you'll be fine."

We moved back by the door and into the sunlight. Bill told me how he had met his wife and gotten married. I wondered if I would ever marry. It seemed like normal things didn't happen to me. There were just crazy things, like people who barked and fights with my father.

Before long, I felt the train slow down. Bill looked out the door.

"This is where I get off," he said. He picked up his pack and gripped my shoulder. "Be careful," he said.

I smiled. "Hope you find her."

He hopped off while the train was still moving, to avoid the railroad yard and the bulls. Looking back, he shot me a grin and a little salute. Then he was gone.

***

I must have fallen asleep, because when I looked up, the train was moving again. The sun was high and the car was empty.

I thought of Bill and the others and wondered if they'd been real. Maybe I had dreamed them. Maybe they were a band of angels, like Daddy preached about from the Bible, sent down to hoist me onto the train and give me travel tips. Remembering Bill's tip, I took the money from my wallet, flattened it, and put it inside my shoe.

The train chugged into the mountains. Suddenly I was tired of crouching in a boxcar and seeing the world framed by a door. Leaning out, I saw a metal ladder going up the side of the car. It reminded me of what Bill had said about walking on top of the train. Part of me was frightened by the idea, but another part was excited. I imagined myself standing on top of the train, arms spread out like I was flying.

I put on my backpack, then took a deep breath and stepped onto the bottom rung of the ladder. The wind whipped by. I steadied myself, gripping the ladder. Rung by rung, I made my way up, making sure that first my hands were in place, then my feet. Finally I pulled myself on top of the car. Standing up, I turned slowly and carefully, taking in the view. It stretched from horizon to horizon, with earth on the bottom and heaven on top. The world was huge and I was hurtling into it.

I started walking, careful to go toward the front, the way Bill had told me to. At first it was hard to keep my balance, but soon I got used to the rocking motion. I imagined it must be something like walking on a boat.

Each time the train reached a curve, I stopped and braced myself, feet wide, leaning forward, then started walking again. When I came to the end of a car, I would sit down, reach forward to the next car, and pull myself across. I got pretty good at it after a while. The train moved, and I moved with it. It was like a living thing, a long metal snake, something Arnie might appreciate.

As I walked, I saw a mountain ahead. The train was moving straight toward it. I stopped and waited, expecting the train to turn aside, but it kept going. The train pounded the rails. The mountain loomed, filling the sky.

Then I saw it. There was a hole in the side of the mountain. It swallowed the train, car by car. The mountain rushed forward. The hole grew. It was a tunnel, deep and dark and bigger by the second.

As I stared, the top of the tunnel rushed toward me, chest high. Gasping, I threw myself onto the roof of the car. Rock hurtled by, inches from my backpack. Smoke billowed and thickened.

The world went black.

CHAPTER 28

The whistle blew. Wheels shrieked on the tracks. The train slowed, then stopped.

I was lying facedown on top of a boxcar. The tunnel was gone. Instead, there was bright sunshine. Bracing my pack, I flopped over onto my side. The hot sun beat down on my cheek. It felt good.

I looked down at my arms. They were black. So were my clothes. I ran a finger along my chin and looked at it. Black.

Once, in the mountains outside of Bristol, I had watched a train go into a tunnel and had wondered where the smoke went. Now I knew. It stayed in the tunnel, packed thick like coal.

My chest heaved, and I pulled out a handkerchief. I coughed into it, and it came away black. The train wasn't just a way to get around. It was part of me, on my body and in my lungs.

"Hey!"

A burly man stood beside the boxcar, pointing up at me. He carried a billy club, the way cops sometimes do. I'd never seen a bull, but I knew without a doubt that this was one.

I looked around and saw that I was in a railroad yard. There were several sets of rails and a couple of trains. A low building stood at one end of the yard, with a sign above it: Gate City.

"Come down off of there," yelled the bull.

I didn't want to get beaten up, and I certainly didn't want my money taken. Checking the other side of the boxcar, I saw a train coming on the next track, and it gave me an idea.

Adjusting my backpack, I climbed to my feet. I strode over and looked off the other side of the car. Sure enough, there was another ladder.

"What are you doing?" shouted the bull.

I scrambled down, missed a rung, and stumbled to the ground. Regaining my balance, I saw the other train approaching on the next track. The engine shrieked and moaned, billowing smoke, as big as a house.

The bull must have climbed into the boxcar and out the other side, because suddenly there he was, right next to me.

Without thinking, without pausing to realize how foolish it was, I lunged across the tracks in front of the other train. The engine rumbled toward me, close enough to touch. The ground shook. I tripped on the rail and then, in desperation, dove. The train thundered past.

I turned and looked back. Between the cars, glimpses of the bull flashed by. He was yelling, but I couldn't hear a thing.

I got up and ran.

***

Gate City was a beautiful place, with a creek flowing through it and mountains all around. I went down to the creek and tried to wash up, without much success. My reflection in the water showed a stranger half-covered with soot.

After I dried off, I headed up a hill to Jackson Street, the main road in town. Checking my reflection in a store window, I ran my fingers through my hair and tried to smooth the wrinkles from my clothes. The first man I saw carried a briefcase and looked like a businessman.

"Excuse me, sir?" I said.

He shot me a look and hurried on around me.

A woman approached, holding a little girl's hand.

"Ma'am?" I said.

She walked right by. The little girl turned and stared at me.

"That man looks bad," she told her mother.

Finally I got tired of being stared at, and I was getting hungry. I headed back down to the creek and turned right, like Bill had said.

I heard it and smelled it before I saw it. There was the rumble of voices and a whiff of unwashed bodies. I rounded a stand of trees, and spread out before me was the jungle, which was more like a village. There must have been a hundred people sitting and talking, clustered in groups of two or three. I saw a couple of tents, but mostly there were coats spread out on the ground and blankets hung from branches.

I picked out a spot under an old oak tree and settled in, leaning against the trunk. The area had been cleared off, and a broken mirror hung from a branch. A boy my age was using it to shave, not that he needed it. His skin was as smooth as mine, but even so there was something rough about him. His sleeves were rolled up, his clothes were dirty, and there was a tired, wary look around his eyes.

He spotted me watching him. "Got a problem?"

"Huh? No, it's nothing."

"You're new, aren't you?"

"How do you know?" I asked.

"Just a guess. Where you from?"

"Bristol."

"I suppose you've seen the jungle there," he said.

"They have one?"

He snorted. "They have hoboes, don't they? They're not staying at the Ritz."

I blushed, embarrassed to know so little about my own town.

"Is there anything to eat?" I asked.

The boy finished shaving and wiped his face with a towel. "Here's how it works. If you bring food, you can take food. Add to the pot, take from the pot."

"Oh."

He studied me. "Of course, maybe you have money."

My hand went to my pocket, and his gaze followed.

"I've got some sausage," he said. "What's it worth to you?"

My mouth watered and my stomach growled. Reaching into my pocket, I felt a few coins.

"How about a nickel?" I asked.

"Sorry." He turned away.

"A dime?"

He looked back at me, then stepped over to another branch, where his pack was hanging. He reached in and pulled out part of a sausage, about the size of my thumb but thicker. Taking a penknife from his pocket, he unfolded the blade and cut the sausage in two.

He showed me one piece. "That's a dime."

I knew for a fact it was worth less than that, but I was hungry. I gave him the dime, and he handed me the sausage. I popped it into my mouth and it was gone, like a drop of water in the ocean.

He stared at me. "Wow, you really are hungry."

That evening, unexpectedly, the weather cooled off. Someone lit a campfire, and everyone gathered around. The heat felt good. As much as anything, though, I think people were drawn by the light. It reflected off their faces, smoothing out the flaws and masking the dirt. In the firelight, they looked like what Daddy might have called a congregation.

The people sang. It wasn't hymns, but there was something holy about it. They had carried the tunes with them and wanted to share—"Black-Eyed Susie," "Pot Licker Blues," "Skip to My Lou." The songs were old, handed down over the years like Grandma's needlepoint or the family Bible. I was sure that, for some of them, it was the only thing they had.

I thought of the hat company and the tunes sung by the

Carters and others. With the help of science, Mr. Peer had re-corded the music, but it was more than that. He had captured their history and traditions.

Gazing into the campfire, I realized that I had a song too. I needed to know what it was and why Mama sang it. The song seemed important, so when there was a break, I sang it, or at least the part I knew. All I got was blank stares.

I remembered the sweetest singer, Sue Dean, and realized that nearly all the voices at the campfire had been male. In the railroad yard, around town, in the jungle, most hoboes were men. That's why, when I headed back from the campfire, I was surprised to hear a female voice.

"No. Don't, please," she was saying.

The voice came from behind a tattered blanket. Setting down my pack, I glanced behind the blanket and saw a big, scruffy man leaning over a young woman. He was holding her, and she was trying to push him away.

"Leave her alone," said another voice. I was surprised to find out it was mine.

The man looked up. "Who are you?"

"I'm her friend," I said, trying to think of something. "The others are coming."

The "others" must have scared him off, because it couldn't have been me. The man let go, backed away, and fled into the bushes.

The young woman looked up at me. For a second she

almost seemed annoyed, then all of that changed. Her face was dirty and her clothes were torn, but there was nothing wrong with her smile.

"If you're my friend, I guess I need to know your name," she said.

"Nate."

"I'm Barbara," she said. "Thank you."

Getting up from the ground, she brushed off her dress, a pretty print with flowers on it. It was the last thing I would have expected in the jungle.

I said, "Don't take this wrong, but you should get some long pants."

"Why?"

I glanced around. "All these men. They might get the wrong idea. Like that one."

"You're sweet," she said. She cocked her head and said, "Real sweet." She was smiling again. Her lips were soft, and her eyes were big. "Do you ever have daydreams?" she asked.

"Yeah, I suppose."

"Here's a nice one." She reached out and touched my arm. "What would happen if we met in normal times? Just you and me, under the trees. I wonder if we'd be sweethearts."

"Sweethearts?"

"I guess we'll never know. Isn't that a shame?" She gave me a peck on the cheek. Then she put her hand on my shoulder, pulled me close, and kissed me.

CHAPTER 29

I was hungry, and not just for food. I wanted company and friendship and the touch of a real, live girl. I kissed her back. It felt good.

There was a noise behind me. A man came out of the bushes, reached around my neck, and squeezed, lifting me off the ground. I smelled bad breath.

"Got him," said the man.

"Good," she said.

Barbara, if that was her name, reached into my pocket and pulled out the coins. She checked the other pockets, found my wallet, and opened it. There was a library card, the photo of Sister's grave, a wildwood flower pressed in waxed paper, but no money. Dropping the wallet, she took my pack and looked inside. She found my pocketknife, then shouldered the pack.

"Don't take it," I gasped. "There's nothing valuable."

"We'll decide that," said Barbara.

"Check his shoes," said the man.

My heart sank. I wondered how he knew. It didn't take long to figure out. Bill's trick might fool the bulls, but hoboes knew.

Barbara yanked off my shoes and took the money.

"Think you're smart, huh?" she said.

She straightened up, opened the knife, and grabbed me by the throat. "Don't follow us. Don't tell anyone. Don't breathe a word. We'll kill you."

Up close, her eyes were flat and dead. Her hands were rough. Her grip was strong, and the knife was sharp. She touched the tip of it to my neck, and I felt a drop of blood trickle down to my shirt.

She said, "Close your eyes. Count to fifty. This never happened."

The man released me. I did as she said. When I opened my eyes, they were gone.

My knees felt weak, and I sank to the ground. I touched my neck. My fingers came away red. I was frightened, but it was more than that. What had just happened? A kiss had turned to blood, comfort to pain, daydream to nightmare. Daddy had always said the line between heaven and hell was just a thread, and it seemed he was right.

How could she do that? I had saved her, hadn't I? Suddenly I realized the answer. I hadn't saved Barbara; I had saved the man who'd been holding her. Barbara's friend had probably been crouched behind a bush, waiting to strike. By chasing off the first man, I had spared him. He still had his pack, if not his pride.

I picked up the wallet and put it back in my pocket. My pack was gone, containing clothes, a toothbrush, a few bandages. All of it was important to me but useless to them. It would end up scattered by the road. Even worse, my money was gone. I was in a strange town, far from home, with nothing but the clothes on my back.

I was cold and hungry. My pack had been the closest thing to a home, and now I really was homeless. Not knowing what else to do, I went back to the campfire. The flames were dying out, and people had drifted away. Curling up near the embers, I fell into a restless sleep.

***

I woke up to shouts in the distance. It wasn't just one person; it was a crowd, and the sound got closer by the minute, moving through the camp. Among the trees, I saw the glint of flashlights and heard the barking of dogs.

The police had come.

"Get up!" they yelled. "Get out!"

I scrambled to my feet just as a young officer approached. "We're not hurting anyone," I told him.

"Just doing what I have to."

"Me too."

"Get your things," he said.

"I don't have any."

He blinked, and I left. I climbed a maple tree beyond the camp and hid in the branches until the police and dogs had swept the area clean, if that's the word for it. The empty camp looked like a trash heap.

When the sun rose, my stomach ached from hunger. I made my way up the hill again and into town, but this time I didn't stop at Jackson Street. I had noticed some big houses farther up the hill. The first one I came to was a tall, yellow structure with two chimneys and a grand entrance. A garage was in back, but I didn't see a car. I noticed tall grass and weeds in the yard, and up close, I noticed the paint was peeling.

I ventured up the steps to the porch and the big front door. I lifted the brass knocker and gave a few taps. The sound rang out. I waited, then knocked again and waited again.

No one answered, so I did what Bill had told me hoboes do—I went to the back door. I knocked, this time with my knuckles. The door opened a crack, and a woman's eye appeared. It was bright blue, with wrinkles around it. The eye blinked and the door opened.

The woman must have been seventy years old. She wore the kind of old-fashioned robe they called a wrapper, with a knit cap on her head and fuzzy slippers, which explained why I hadn't heard her coming. She had a kind face and a welcoming smile.

"Thank you for opening the door," I said. "I was just wondering if you could spare some food. Table scraps, anything."

She studied me. "You're filthy. You need food. Would you like to come in?"

On the train, Bill had told me about handouts. He said they fell into three categories. A lump was food in a bag, which you had to take somewhere else. A knee-shaker was food on a tray, so you could eat sitting on the back step. And a sit-down, the rarest of all handouts, was food at the table, when you were invited inside. This would be a sit-down, on my very first try.

"Yes, ma'am," I said, trying not to sound too eager. "Could I?"

"Not if you keep standing there."

CHAPTER 30

The woman turned and headed into the kitchen. I followed, shutting the door behind me.

It was a big kitchen, the kind where servants might have worked. There were no servants now, just an old woman drawing water at the sink.

"Tea?" she asked.

"Uh, yes. Please."

Next to the sink was the biggest stove I'd ever seen. As long as a good-sized couch, the stove had a white enamel finish, three oven doors, and six burners with a knob for each. The woman set the teapot on a burner and turned a knob. She saw me gaping and smiled.

"I used to be rich," she said. "Can you tell?"

Across from the stove was another big appliance, with a couple of latched doors on the front.

"That's a Frigidaire," she told me. "In 1925 it was the best icebox money could buy. We had lots of money, my husband and I. Then his business went bad, and he killed himself."

"I'm sorry," I mumbled.

She waved her hand. "Spilt milk. Can't do nothing about it."

Looking me up and down, she said, "You're tired. Sit down."

The kitchen table was long and sturdy. I moved to one end of it and settled in. After spending the night on the hard ground, the wooden chair seemed almost soft.

She opened the Frigidaire and pulled out a couple of dishes with tinfoil on them.

"There's sausage and potato salad," she said, transferring some of the food to a plate. She put it in front of me, along with silverware and a paper napkin.

I ate a few bites, trying not to wolf it all down. I couldn't tell you if it was good, because it was going down so fast.

She watched me eat. "I'm Dolly. What's your name?"

"Nate," I managed between bites. "Nate Owens."

"You're hungry," she said.

I blushed. "Yes, ma'am."

"You're hungry and I'm blunt," said Dolly. "Somewhere between the suicide and the funeral, I got tired of pussyfooting around. Just woke up one morning and thought, I'm gonna say what's on my mind. If they don't like it, too bad."

She leaned forward. "Here's the deal. I'm not rich anymore, but I have some money. Others don't. So I share. When folks come around, I let them in. I feed them. All I ask is that they pass it on—the kindness, not the food."

For a minute, I wondered if she was going to ask me to pray. She must have noticed my concern.

"No conditions," she said. "No strings attached. Just do good. Don't hit people. Don't steal their things. Treat 'em right. That's it."

I nodded, my mouth stuffed with food. I'd heard a lot of sermons, but that one may have been the best.

She pushed the dishes toward me. "Keep eating. Plenty more where that came from."

The teapot whistled, and Dolly poured two cups of tea. She sipped hers in silence and watched me eat. It took a while. Somewhere around my third plateful, she finished her tea and excused herself for a minute.

"Dang bladder," she said. "Size of an acorn."

She had brought me into the kitchen through the back. Now she headed the other way, opening a door into what looked like the dining room. As she did, I heard the faint sound of music. But it wasn't just any music. It was the Carters, playing on a phonograph.

Out in the cold world and far away from home
Somebody's boy is wandering alone
No one to guide him and keep his footsteps right
Somebody's boy is homeless tonight

Bring back my boy, my wandering boy
Far, far away, wherever he may be
Tell him his mother, with faded cheeks and hair
At their old home is waiting him there

I was back in Bristol at the hat company. Sara was singing, and Maybelle was strumming her guitar in that odd, wonderful way of hers. There was a little catch in Sara's voice, and now I heard it again. This was one of the records they had made that day. I hadn't realized it at the time, but just a year later, the song would be about me.

I thought of Mama waiting at home, maybe washing dishes, not knowing where I was. I hadn't told her goodbye. I'd been afraid that if I had, I wouldn't have been able to leave. Daddy had always been shout and bluster. He prayed out loud for everyone to hear. Mama stayed in the background. But every meal she cooked, every sock she darned, every face she scrubbed—those were prayers too. She was praying for me now. I could feel it.

When Dolly came back, she walked over and put her hand on my shoulder.

"You're crying," she said.

That's just the way she was. If she saw it, she said it. She was like Mr. Peer's recording machine, walking around on two legs.

She waited patiently. My feelings leaked out. I'd been holding them in—on the train, through the mountains, in the town, and, truth be told, at home before I'd ever left. Daddy had always shared his feelings with everyone. Mama and I kept ours inside. Arnie was like Daddy, and I was like Mama. I could see that now. The only difference was I'd been able to leave.

I wiped my eyes on a napkin, and it came away smudged with black. Dolly went into the other room, and a minute later I heard another record, "Keep on the Sunny Side."

When Dolly came back, I told her, "I know them. The Carters."

She picked up the dishes and took them to the sink. "We all know them."

"You do?"

"Well, around here at least. I see A.P. in town sometimes. They live in Poor Valley, just up the road."

I started to tell her about meeting them in Bristol, but suddenly it didn't matter. The Carters weren't some distant memory. They were real, and they lived nearby. They were singing in the other room—calling me, just as surely as if they had picked up a telephone.

"Can you tell me how to get there?" I asked. "I might want to say hi."

"Easiest way is by train. Go east one stop. Get off at Neal's store. That's Poor Valley. A.P. bought a new house there last year when they got back from New Jersey. Folks say they used their recording profits. Imagine, singing for money."

I got up from the table. "Thank you for the food. And for everything."

Dolly started to hug me, then stepped back. "My God, you're dirty. It's all right though. You seem like a good boy."

***

I hopped a freight train, this time headed east. A short time after I got on, the train slowed down again. I looked ahead and saw what looked like a store, so I picked a spot and jumped off. I had to admit, I was getting pretty good at it.

The train came to a stop, then rumbled on again, around the bend, and up into the mountains. The store I'd seen had a sign on top: Neal's. People were milling around—neighbors visiting, children laughing, folks playing checkers in front. I crossed the railroad tracks and mounted the steps. I got a few looks, but nobody said anything.

Inside, the place was as big as Daddy's tent, which was large by anybody's standards. There was a counter with prices posted for train tickets and another one for US mail. In the center was a potbellied stove. A table was set up next to it, and four old men were playing cards. Daddy said cards were Satan's tools, but I always thought they looked like fun.

I walked over and stood nearby, trying to see what the men were doing. One of them glanced up and eyed me.

"Help you?" he asked.

"It's okay," I said. "Don't mind me."

A little while later, he pulled his cards to his chest and glanced up at me again. "Looking for something? Cause it ain't in this hand."

"Sorry," I stammered. I decided to plunge in. "I heard the Carter Family lives around here. Is that true?"

"Who wants to know?" he asked.

The man across from him smiled. "Don't mind Horace," he told me. "He gets like that when he's losing."

"I ain't losing," said Horace.

"The Carters live just down the hill," said the other man. "Step outside and look for a house with a cedar tree in front. Can't miss it."

I nodded. "Much obliged."

"Anyway," said the man, "we all know what Horace is holding—diddly squat."

The other men laughed, and I moved off toward the door. On the way I passed some barrels filled with candy and nuts. It was all I could do to keep from reaching out and grabbing some.

I went through the front door and looked down the hill. Sure enough, I saw a house with a cedar tree. The house wasn't as large as Dolly's, but for Poor Valley, I figured it qualified as big.

Walking down the hill, I studied the place. The house itself was square with a pointed roof. It was unpainted, so it blended in with the hillside. A porch with six pillars stretched across the front, making it seem wider than it was, and a creek ran along the back with an outhouse next to it. The house didn't seem like the sort of place where anyone famous lived. For that matter, the Carters didn't seem famous. They were just regular people. Maybe that's why folks liked them.

It was one of those warm fall days, so the front door was open, leaving just the screen door. I took a deep breath, crossed the porch, and knocked. A figure appeared behind the screen.

It was Sue Dean.

PART V

DON'T FORGET
THIS SONG

My home's in old Virginia among the lovely hills
The memory of my birthplace lies in my bosom still
I did not like my fireside, I did not like my home
I have a mind for rambling so far away from home

—A. P. Carter, "Don't Forget This Song"

CHAPTER 31

She was holding a little boy who was a year or two old. Wearing an apron, she was as pretty as ever. Her hair was red. Freckles dotted her face, like I remembered. I had traced them with my finger.

I realized the little boy was Joe, who had been a baby the last time I'd seen him. Peeking out from behind Sue Dean's skirt was a dark-haired girl maybe five years older than Joe, and beyond her was Gladys, who had grown a few inches but was still short.

"Yes?" said Sue Dean.

I must have looked pretty different. I felt different too. There was the soot, of course, but maybe there were other things.

"It's Nate," I said.

Her eyes widened. "Oh my God."

As quickly as it came, amazement was replaced by something else. It was cold and hard. The last time she'd seen me I'd made a promise, and I had broken it.

In my mind, I had imagined this moment over and over

again. Now that the time had arrived, all I could do was stand there. We stared at each other through the screen.

Someone came up behind her. It was Sara.

"Mama," said Gladys, "it's Sue Dean's friend, Nate. You know, the boy from Bristol."

"Sorry to bother you," I said, finding my tongue. "I've been...traveling. I heard your records and decided to say hello. I didn't expect to find Sue Dean."

Sara squinted through the screen, then smiled. "I remember you."

"Your records are beautiful," I told her.

"You helped make them," said Gladys. "Didn't he, Mama?"

Sara pushed open the screen door. "Don't just stand out there. Come on in."

I glanced at Sue Dean. She didn't seem too keen on the idea.

Sara didn't notice. "Come on, now," she told me.

I nodded my thanks and stepped inside. The room was simple and well kept, with magazines on the table and pansies in a vase. A stone fireplace took up one wall, and on the mantel was a lantern. Apparently, electricity hadn't come to Poor Valley.

Little Joe squirmed out of Sue Dean's arms, came up beside me, and wrinkled his nose. "He smells."

"Shush!" hissed Sara. "He's our guest."

Meanwhile, Sue Dean studied me, the way you'd study an insect.

"We're about to have our midday dinner," said Sara. "Can you join us?"

I looked at Sue Dean again. This time hunger won out over guilt.

"Yes'm. I'd like that."

"It'll be ready in a few minutes," she said, eyeing Sue Dean. "You all probably have some catching up to do."

Sara headed for the kitchen, and her parade followed. Gladys kept looking back at me.

Sue Dean pushed open the screen door, and I followed her outside. I sat on the porch swing and expected her to join me. Instead she stood over me, arms crossed.

"You hurt me," she said.

For three years I had dreaded those words.

"I didn't mean to," I told her.

"Don't whine," she snapped. "When you feel bad, you whine."

"I do?"

"I needed to see you. I wanted to say goodbye. You didn't let me. Why didn't you come?"

There was pain in her voice. She deserved an answer.

I said, "Remember Beelzebub? The rattler?"

"I suppose."

"That night at the service, it bit Arnie. They took him to the hospital. He lived, but just barely."

She stared at me.

"Maybe it sounds like whining," I said, "but with Arnie hurt and everything, I forgot. That's the truth, Sue Dean. I forgot."

She closed her eyes, then sighed and sat down beside me.

"I'm sorry about your brother," she said. "But it was important. I thought we were friends."

"When I got to the cabin, I saw your note. I didn't know your father was in trouble."

"We had to go away," she said. "I waited for you as long as I could."

"You could have sent me your address."

"There wasn't one. We had no idea where we were going. Then later, when we had one, I didn't want to."

I winced, knowing I deserved it. "How did you end up here?" I asked.

"We went to Virginia. Mama and Daddy kept fighting. Daddy was looking for another factory job but couldn't find one. Finally he gave up, so we got a little place and tried farming. Daddy was no good at it. It made him mad. Everything made him mad. He and Mama would fight, and I'd try to imagine a happy family. I recalled that I'd seen one, even been part of it for a few days."

"The Carters," I said.

She nodded. "They were famous by then. What I remembered best was those children. I wondered if Sara still needed help. I packed my bags, and a few days later I found them. I miss Mama and Daddy, but I'm happy to be here."

"What are you going to do?" I asked.

"I'm doing it."

"I mean eventually."

"I don't know," she said. "I haven't thought that far ahead."

I said, "So I guess we both left home."

"I guess."

Maybe she didn't want to hear why I left, but I wanted to tell her.

"The snake escaped. People were afraid to come back, and the church shut down. Things got bad at home. Daddy and I had a fight."

"Did you keep going to the cabin?"

I shook my head. "That was our place, not mine."

I thought that might catch her interest, but she just looked away.

I said, "After you left, Mr. Lane kept firing people. He blocked the union. I told him he was a terrible person."

Sue Dean looked up.

"So, he fired me," I said. "Like he fired your father."

"Good," she said.

It seemed that I couldn't do anything right, no matter how hard I tried.

"I messed things up," I told her. "I'm still messing up. But I'm glad you're here." I looked out at the yard and the fields and the mountains beyond. I said, "It's good to see the Carters again. I love their music."

"'Single Girl, Married Girl,'" she said. "That's my favorite."

"You know what my favorite is?"

I took out my wallet, removed the waxed paper, and opened it. There, dried out, breaking apart, was a lily with six pointed petals, orange at the center and red on the tips.

"'Wildwood Flower,'" I said.

She gazed at it. Then she turned away, got to her feet, and went inside.

CHAPTER 32

I followed Sue Dean inside, and we sat at the rough kitchen ta-ble. I was pretty sure the table, along with most of the house, had started out as trees on the hill above Neal's. Settling in, I told myself this wasn't a sit-down, like at Dolly's house. It seemed different, more like visiting friends.

As Sara finished cooking the meal, Gladys opened the icebox and poured me a glass of buttermilk. It was cold and thick. I tried to sip it, not gulp it. The children stood around me in a circle, watching.

Sara laughed. "He's a guest, not a monkey in the zoo."

Gladys sat down across from me. Joe climbed up on Sue Dean's lap, alongside the little, dark-haired girl.

"I'm Janette," said the girl. "I wish Mama had let me come to Bristol. I want to see how they make records."

"It's like magic," Gladys told her.

"It's science," I said. The word sounded good, like an old companion. "There's a microphone, an amplifier, and a lathe. The lathe cuts a groove. That's where the music is."

I heard the screen door slam in the front room, and a

man's voice called out, "Where's my dinner?"

Sara, stirring a pot on the stove, chuckled and glanced over at me. "I should have warned you, you're not the only guest."

The kitchen door swung open, and a man in uniform strode in. He had a funny way of walking, with his hands held out by his hips. He wore blue pants, a neatly pressed shirt and tie, and a matching coat with a double row of buttons. On his head was a hat with a shiny black visor, and a badge was pinned to his lapel. For a minute, I wondered if he was the sheriff, come to arrest me.

He took off the hat, revealing hair that sat in waves above a strong, handsome face. There was something familiar about him, but I couldn't place what it was. When he saw me, he stopped short.

"Who's this?" he asked Sara.

"Nate Owens. He helped us in Bristol."

With the word *Bristol*, I figured it out.

"Virgie Hobbs," I told Sara, "that relative you stayed with in town. He looks just like her."

"Correction," said the man. "She looks just like me."

Sara grinned. "This is A.P.'s younger brother Ezra. We call him Eck. He and Virgie are twins. She's older by a few minutes."

"Yeah," said Eck, "she popped out first to tell everyone I was coming."

I stood up and offered my hand. He hesitated for the

barest minute, and I thought of his fine uniform next to my tattered clothes. Then he smiled and shook my hand.

"Glad to meet you. Thanks for helping my brother. Lord knows he can use it."

I thought of the gangly, awkward man who had sung with Sara and Maybelle and seemed like he was filled with music.

"Is he going to be here?" I asked.

Eck looked out the window at the autumn colors. "A.P.? He's like those leaves. Will they fall? Yes. Do we know where or when? Not likely."

He sat down in a chair next to me, and I studied his uniform. "Are you in the army?"

"Sure," he said with a wink. "The postal army."

He took the badge from his lapel and plopped it into my hand. It was polished silver, with an eagle perched on top. In the middle was a big *US*, and around the edges were the words *Post Office Department—Railway Mail Service.*

Gladys piped up. "Uncle Eck rides the trains. He sorts mail for the whole area."

"I've been blessed," said Eck. "I'm lucky to have work in tough times. We all are." He glanced in my direction and caught himself. "You'd be happy to work too. I know you would."

"Yes, sir," I said.

"Uncle Eck's an important man," Gladys said.

"In his mind," said Sara.

Eck shook his head and smirked. "No respect."

I thought of the odd way he moved, with his hands held out by his hips, and figured it must have been from walking on the train, steadying himself on the seat backs.

Watching him, I searched my memory. "They told us about you. It was your car they were driving. You're Maybelle's husband."

"I like this kid," Eck said. "He knows all the important stuff."

The kitchen door swung open again and Maybelle entered carrying a basket full of shucked corn in one arm and a baby in the other. The last time I'd seen Maybelle, she'd had a big belly and no children. Obviously the baby had been born after they got home from Bristol.

"I guess you know Maybelle," Eck told me. "And that's little Helen."

He took Helen from Maybelle and leaned down close to her. "Come on, sweetheart. Give your daddy some sugar."

Helen kissed him, and he handed her to Sue Dean. Maybelle gave the basket to Sara, who put the corn into a big pot of boiling water.

Maybelle turned to me. "Nate, isn't it? Good to see you again. What are you doing here?"

"Eating, if we ever give him a chance," said Sara.

It turned out that Eck had a midday break between mail runs. He said he had stopped by to get reacquainted with his family, but it seemed to me he might have come for the corn.

When Sara boiled it and brought it to the table, along with the rest of the food, he finished off three ears before saying another word. Then he said lots of them.

Eck filled me in on family history, which with the Carters seemed as important as the food on the table. Eck, A.P., Virgie, and their five brothers and sisters had grown up in a little cabin in Poor Valley, raising tobacco and hogs. Sara and her cousin Maybelle came from the other side of Clinch Mountain, the high ridge behind Neal's, in a place called Copper Creek. Cousins married brothers, making a tangled-up family where a girl like Gladys turned out to be her own cousin.

"Now, I'll tell you about A.P.," Eck said. "He's not here, so it's a perfect chance. Besides, I'm his brother, so I'm allowed. His name's Alvin Pleasant Delaney Carter, but we call him Pleasant or Doc. He's odd, you know—but in a good way. They say when Mama was pregnant with him, she stood under an apple tree in a thunderstorm and the tree was struck by lightning. Yessir, zap! When he popped out a few months later, he shook."

"Shook?" I asked.

"You know, trembled. His hands, his voice—kids used to tease him something awful. He didn't care though. Doc was in his own world, dreaming about music. He used to walk the railroad tracks, hands behind his back, just thinking and humming. Still does. Craziest thing. It's a wonder he hasn't been squashed like a bug.

"Doc, well, he's what folks around here call 'wifty'—you know, strung a little tight. Besides being odd, he's stubborn and has a temper. He picked up a fiddle when he was little, and first thing you know, he played a song, 'Johnny Get Your Hair Cut Short.' Pretty soon he was singing—at church, in the parlor, on the railroad tracks. Beautiful voice, everybody knows it. Now the world knows it. They've sold thousands of records. Ain't that something?"

After dinner, the kids scrambled down from the table and played games on the floor with Sue Dean. Maybelle got her guitar, Sara set out some blackberry cobbler, and we had the finest time eating and listening to music.

Around about the second piece of cobbler and the third tune, I heard the sound of a car engine. Gladys jumped up and ran to the window.

"It's Daddy!" she said.

I came up beside her and looked out. A red Chevrolet was parked in front, and the unmistakable form of A. P. Carter stood beside it. Next to him, just as cool as could be, was a young Negro man.

CHAPTER 33

Gladys ran out the door with Janette and Joe behind her. Sara and Sue Dean went with them, and so did I. When Joe got to the car, he threw himself at A.P.'s leg and hugged it.

"Hello, sweet boy," said A.P. in that deep, quivery voice. He looked over at me and cocked his head, like he was thinking.

Sara said, "Doc, you remember Nate Owens? You met him in Bristol."

"Well, ain't that something," said A.P., smiling vaguely.

The young Negro man reached into the car and picked up a crutch. When he turned around, I saw why. His right leg was missing from the knee down.

He smiled at me. "Lost that leg in a cement factory. Been looking for it ever since."

His face was the color of Mama's coffee when she put cream in it. He had a thin mustache and the hint of a beard on his chin. He wasn't exactly handsome, but he looked friendly.

"I'm Lesley Riddle," he said. "Folks call me Esley."

Little Joe tugged on A.P.'s trousers. Gladys said, "Daddy, there's food."

A.P. took Joe's hand, and they headed for the house. Sara, Sue Dean, and the girls went along, telling him the latest news. Esley and I followed.

Inside, Sara dished up some dinner for A.P. and Esley. The girls gathered around A.P., talking excitedly. Esley took his plate and joined me on the couch. In between bites, he looked up at me.

"You were in Bristol? Did you see Doc and them make the records?"

I nodded. "I even learned how the recording machines worked."

Esley said, "You like machines?"

"Sure do."

"We got a machine," said Esley, breaking off a piece of cornbread. He nodded toward the window. "That car of A.P.'s."

"I used to work on cars," I told him.

Esley studied me, surprised. "You did? You think you could fix ours? Doc and me, we do better with music than cars."

I looked out the window at the Chevrolet. It might be dirty, but it was the latest model. "What's the problem?"

"Doc bought it with some of their record money. I swear, something's always going wrong." Esley shook his head. "Maybe it was that boiler."

"What boiler?"

"Well, you see, Doc was hunting songs in North Carolina when he found a sawmill boiler for sale. Rock-bottom price. Couldn't pass it up. So he bought the boiler, chained it to the bumper, and dragged it home. Two hundred miles, across mountains and dirt roads."

"With the Chevrolet?"

Esley nodded. "Brand-new, or at least it was. Then there was the hog."

"Hog?"

"Doc's sow had a date with a stud hog—you know, to make pigs. Problem was, he didn't have a way to get her there. So he pulled up the Chevrolet, took out the back seat, and shoved in the sow."

I tried to imagine A.P. wrestling the sow, but I just couldn't do it. I asked Esley, "You said the car needs to be fixed. What's wrong?"

"I'll show you," he said.

Esley finished eating, then set the plate by the sink and took me out to the car. Using the crutch like part of his body, he hobbled to the driver's side, sat behind the wheel, and started the engine.

"Sounds smooth, right?" he said. "But when you move, it bucks like a bronco. Get in—you'll see."

I climbed in front, and he took me for a ride. It was amazing to watch him drive. He did everything with his left foot—gas, clutch, brake. There was something graceful about it, like a dance. But there was nothing graceful in how the car drove. As we sped up, there was a pinging sound, then a vibration. Then, sure enough, it started bucking.

"What do you think?" he asked.

"That's not the engine," I told him. "It's the drive train. I'll take a look at it."

Esley headed back inside, while I found the owner's manual under the front seat and started reading. A.P.'s Chevrolet was different from the Packard, but not that much.

As I finished reading, Eck came out the front door of the house, putting on his postman's hat. "Got a mail run," he told me. "My train's coming through pretty soon."

"You know where I can find some tools?" I asked.

"Are you going to fix the car?"

"I'll try."

He nodded toward a shed behind the house. "There's a few in there," he said. "I use them myself sometimes. Lord knows they can't be Doc's. Maybe the last folks left them behind."

He took me to the shed, where I found a jack and some wrenches.

"Can I help?" he asked. "I have a few minutes yet."

"It's okay. I'm used to working by myself. Besides, you don't want to get your uniform dirty."

Eck watched while I jacked up the car and crawled underneath. After poking around a while, I found the problem.

"A bad U-joint," I told him. "It's simple to fix, but I'll need a part."

"I'm in Roanoke this afternoon. Tell me what you want, and I'll get it. Then, when I come back tomorrow, you can do the repair."

He gave me a pen. I took the owner's manual from the car, circled the part, then handed him the pen and manual.

"Much obliged," I said.

"How old did you say you were?"

I managed a smile. It felt funny, like I was out of practice.

"I didn't," I said, "but I'm fourteen."

"How did you learn this stuff?"

I shrugged. "I like science. And I worked for a while as a mechanic."

Eck nodded, then folded up the owner's manual and stuck it in his coat pocket. "See you tomorrow," he said.

CHAPTER 34

Maybelle and Helen went home after dinner. Sue Dean put Joe down for a nap, then she and Sara took the girls off to do some chores. A.P. and Esley stayed behind, so they could work on the blackberry cobbler.

Gladys looked back at me as she left the room. She told Sue Dean, "We have a guest. Shouldn't we stay and visit?"

"We have two guests," said Sue Dean, glancing at Lesley Riddle.

Gladys giggled. "That's not a guest. That's Esley."

After they left, I moved to the table for cobbler and another glass of buttermilk, which Esley got for me. The buttermilk was cold and thick, so good it seemed sinful.

"I've heard your records," I told A.P. "You sell lots of them."

A smile played across his face, but it wasn't aimed at me. It was his, from some private place inside of him.

"Yes, sir," he warbled.

"Must be great," I said.

He shrugged. "Life's not so different from before. But now we have some nice things, like the house."

"And the car, if you can fix it," added Esley.

A.P. went on, "Main thing is, now I don't have to work at the sawmill or sell fruit trees. I can do my music."

"You mean concerts? Records?"

"More than that," said A.P. "That's the giving. I'm talking about the getting."

Sometimes A.P. spoke in code. He'd done it a few times in Bristol. It was like he had a language of his own inside his head.

"What's the getting?" I asked.

Esley grinned. "That's where I come in."

"He helps me remember," said A.P.

I looked at Esley, confused.

Esley laughed. "You don't know what he's talking about, do you?"

I shook my head.

Esley said, "You were in Bristol. You know why the Carters went there."

"To make records?"

"Well, sure," he said. "But why?"

I tried to figure it out. Finally I shrugged.

"Mr. Peer pays fifty dollars a song," said Esley. "It's why all those people came. A.P. wants more songs and knows where to get them."

"In the hollers," A.P. grunted.

The hollers were what local people called the hidden valleys or hollow places between mountain ridges.

A.P. leaned forward over the cobbler. His shirt brushed the blackberries and got a smudge, but he didn't care. His eyes were bright, and the vague expression was gone.

"The people hold on to their songs—the old songs, the ones they brought across the ocean years ago," he said with feeling. "They keep them and sing them and pass them down, generation to generation."

I recalled the jungle in Gate City, where hoboes sat around the fire, singing the one thing they still had.

"If you ask people, they'll play their songs for you," A.P. said.

"You collect them?" I asked.

"Yes, sir."

"And the people don't mind?"

"Mind?" he said. "They're thrilled to death. The Carter family wants their songs!"

"Anyway, he doesn't just take the songs," said Esley. "He changes 'em. He tucks 'em in here, let's 'em out there, adds a chorus or verse. He makes harmonies. By the time he's done, the songs are the same but different. They've been Carterized."

"Where do you come in?" I asked.

Esley smiled. "Like he said, I help him remember. You know how parrots repeat whatever you say? Well, I do that with songs."

"It's a fact," said A.P. "He remembers tunes. Knows

hundreds of them, maybe thousands. See, when I started in the hollers, I wrote down the words but forgot the notes. Then I met Esley here. Notes were his specialty. Now I write down the words and he learns the melodies."

A.P. lurched to his feet, knocking the table back and tipping over the chair. He reached into his pockets, pulled out handfuls of paper scraps, and spilled them onto the table like confetti.

"See those?" he said. "Every one is a song. I tear off paper from notepads, envelopes, telephone books. I write down the words, but the music is in here." He reached out and tapped the side of Esley's head.

Esley didn't seem to mind. He just smiled.

Esley carried songs around in his head. I knew what that felt like. I thought of my song, the one I'd heard in the night, the one Mama had sung. I wondered if Esley knew it.

***

I stayed for supper, and when it got dark, A.P. headed for bed. Sue Dean went to tuck in the girls.

Sara cleaned up the kitchen, then turned to me. "You'll spend the night?"

"You've been so nice," I said. "You don't have to do that."

"Course we do. Anyway, you need to be here tomorrow when the part comes in. You help us; we help you. That's the way it works."

"Thank you, ma'am."

After she left, Esley took his guitar from its beat-up case and started strumming. At first, I thought he might wake up the family. Then I realized that at the Carters' house, the sound of a guitar must be as natural as the breeze.

The tunes poured out of him—happy, sad, angry, lonesome. I closed my eyes and listened. In the darkness behind my eyes, a melody formed, as it always did. The words followed, and when Esley stopped, I sang them. He listened intently, then played along on his guitar. It was Mama's song.

I stared at him. "You know that?"

He stopped and gazed through the window, off into the distance. "I'm not sure. It seems familiar."

"Could you sing the rest? I just heard that one verse."

He closed his eyes and concentrated, then sighed and shook his head. "Sorry. It was a long time ago. Maybe when I was a kid in North Carolina."

Hearing him say it sent a shiver up my back. "Where in North Carolina?"

"Burnsville, near the Tennessee border. I was born there."

I remembered conversations from my own childhood, questions I had asked Mama and Daddy about North Carolina. All they would tell me was a town.

"I was born in Deep Gap," I told him. "Is that anywhere close?"

"Not far," said Esley. "Fifty, sixty miles, over in Watauga County."

My song was just a fragment, but now it had a place— Watauga County, in North Carolina. Esley had heard it. Maybe others had too. It was a pretty song, but in my family, it caused pain. That night in the kitchen, I'd seen the pain in Mama's face, felt it in her voice.

Sitting there with Esley, I thought about the pain—where it had come from and why I had left. My past, held back for so long, came crashing in on me, and suddenly I needed to tell it.

"Want to hear a story?" I asked Esley.

He nodded, and it occurred to me that Esley's real gift, with music or stories, was listening.

I started in the kitchen that night hearing the song and worked my way out, to the family, to the house, to the tent. I described Daddy's church and the snake and the healings that stirred folks up but didn't necessarily make them better. I told him about the preacher who lit up like a torch, the woman who stood beside him, the boy who had been damaged, and the boy who had escaped. I told him about a church that didn't have music and trains that did.

When I finished, the room was quiet for a while.

Finally, Esley said, "That's quite a story."

"Sometimes I hate it," I told him. "Sometimes it makes me ache."

"That church—it really didn't have music?"

"Never."

"But why?"

I had to admit I didn't know.

Esley pondered that for a minute. "What you told me—it's not just a story. It's a mystery."

He strummed for a while longer, then hobbled over and opened a closet. "Here's a couple of blankets. You take the couch. I'll sleep on the floor."

"Really? The floor?"

"Hey, I do it all the time."

I thought for a minute, then shook my head. "The couch is yours. I've got someplace else in mind."

He handed me a blanket. Moving to the front door, I opened it and stepped across the big porch to the front yard. The moon was high. There was a nip in the air. Crickets sang, and somewhere a bullfrog croaked. Mountains ringed the valley, wrapping around me like Mama's arms.

I walked to the Chevrolet, opened the front door, and stretched out on the seat. It felt like home.

CHAPTER 35

There was more food the next morning—eggs, grits, sausage, toast. At first I was embarrassed at how much I ate, but Sara liked watching me.

"It's a compliment," she said, bringing out more eggs. I took a couple and passed them on to A.P. and Esley.

Sue Dean helped Joe with his food, while Gladys and Janelle finished up. When they were done, Sue Dean took them out to the front porch to jump rope. I wanted to talk with her, but I didn't think she'd like that.

"I'll be doing a load of clothes at the creek," Sara said. "If you give me yours, I'll wash them."

I looked down at my shirt and pants, caked with soot. "These are all I've got. What'll I wear?"

"Doc has some extra clothes," she said. "You can wear his to fix the car. That way, yours will stay clean once I wash them."

Clean. It was a word I hadn't thought much about lately.

"When you're done with the car, you can take a bath," said Sara. "I'll get out the tub. Doc can draw water at the well, and I'll heat some up for you."

"Are you sure?" I asked.

"I'd advise it," she said with a twinkle in her eye.

I changed into some of A.P.'s clothes, rolling up the long legs and sleeves. A little while later, Eck came back. His uniform looked as neat as ever. I couldn't tell if he had changed it on the train or if that's just the way he was.

"Here's the U-joint," he said, handing me a bag. "And hey, I like that outfit."

"Sara was doing some wash. I gave her my clothes."

He raised his eyebrows. "Today's Thursday. Sara washes on Saturday."

I gazed at him, then we both laughed.

"Did she say anything about a bath?" he asked.

I nodded. "As soon as the car's fixed. I guess I'm pretty dirty, huh?"

"Only your friends will tell you," said Eck.

A couple of hours later, the new part was in place, and the Chevrolet was fixed. When A.P. brought water from the well, I used some of it to wash the car. Under all the dirt, it was shiny and nice.

Esley stood by, admiring the car. He turned to A.P. "Ready to roll?" he said. "Find some more songs?"

"I reckon," said A.P.

Esley pulled a map from the glove compartment and opened it on the hood of the car.

"I was thinking," he said, "we haven't been to North

Carolina for a while."

My heart gave a little hop.

"What about Mandy Groves's friend?" said A.P.

Esley turned to me and explained, "Amanda Groves lives across the river from here. Big, tall lady with bright-red hair. If you're digging for songs, she's the mother lode. When A.P. started out, he just sat on her porch and she'd sing to him. She told A.P. about a friend in North Carolina."

"Let's see," A.P. warbled, "where was it she lived?"

"Watauga County," said Esley.

Just like that, the world opened up. My song played. The mystery beckoned, stretching back to our kitchen and Daddy's tent and the strange faith he had dreamed up where music was a sin. Esley nodded to me, and I knew I'd be going with them. It was just a matter of how.

With the car repairs done, Sara took the rest of the water, heated it up, and poured it into a galvanized tub. She hung some blankets around the tub, handed me a bar of lye soap, and said, "Have at it."

I pulled the blankets closed and took off my clothes, or rather A.P.'s, then stepped in and scrubbed. The water turned black and filled up with the most amazing things, which apparently I'd been carrying around on my body. They weren't as bad as Daddy's snake, but a couple of them came close.

Eck stayed for dinner. Later that afternoon, after my clothes had dried, I put them on and made an appearance at the porch, where Eck was talking with A.P. and Esley. I had to admit, I felt like a new man, or at least a new boy.

"What do you think?" I asked them.

"He's human," said Eck.

Eck shot A.P. a look, and A.P. cleared his throat. "We been talking."

Esley broke in. "Mostly Eck's been talking. But we liked what he said."

"Seems you need a job," A.P. told me. "Is that right?"

"Yes, sir."

"Well, maybe you noticed—Esley and me, we're not so good with cars. But, well…you are." A.P. fidgeted, then looked at Eck and back at me. "Ah, the heck with it. I'm no good with words. We have car trouble. Want to be our mechanic?"

I stared at him. "You mean, stay here and work on the car?"

"Not stay here," said Esley. "Come with us to collect songs. When the car breaks down, you can fix it."

"Yes," I blurted before they could change their minds.

A.P. went on. "Of course, we'll pay you, and—what did you say?"

"Yes!"

Eck grinned.

A.P. leaned back. "Well, that was quick."

"Told you," said Esley.

***

Afterward, I wondered about Sue Dean. I had found her, and now I was leaving again. It seemed bad, but in another way, maybe it was good. She was angry. Maybe she needed some time to think.

Anyway, I didn't have a chance to consider it, because A.P. was anxious to get going. He and Esley packed up after supper that night. Sara gave me a satchel so I could pack too.

"What do I put in it?" I asked her.

"Just wait," she told me.

She led me to a little room down the hall. There she showed me another machine, but this one was for inside work, not outside. At first I thought it was just an oak table with iron legs. Then she opened up the top and pulled out a familiar object, like one that Mama had at home but fancier, painted black with gold decorations and the word Singer on the side. It was a sewing machine.

"Ain't she a beauty?" asked Sara.

"Yes, ma'am," I said.

"When we got paid for those songs, A.P. bought a car. I bought this. Here, take a look."

Pulling up a chair, she showed me how it worked. What I had thought were just iron legs turned out to be the engine that drove it. There was a flat, metal place to put your foot— Sara called it a treadle—and when you pumped it, a wheel spun and the needle went up and down. She took a scrap of cloth from one of the drawers, stretched it out flat under the needle, and pumped the treadle. A line of stitches appeared on that cloth just as straight as it could be.

"Now, let's get you something to put in that satchel," she said.

She disappeared into her bedroom and came out with an armful of clothes. "These are some extras that A.P. doesn't use anymore."

Holding them up next to me, she measured the sleeves and pant legs, then sat down and went to work. An hour later, I had some clothes. I tried them on and they fit, thanks to Sara's machine. I had clothes to choose from for the first time since the girl named Barbara had stolen my pack. She had taken everything I had, and now Sara was giving some of it back.

The next morning, Sara cooked breakfast bright and early. Then she and Sue Dean filled a basket with food for us to take. Esley loaded it into the car, alongside a couple of suitcases, the guitar, his crutch, and my satchel.

Sara and the children stood nearby. Sue Dean held Joe, and the girls clasped hands.

"Well, Doc," said Sara, "here you go again."

"Yes'm," he grunted.

"Seems like you're gone a lot."

It occurred to me that while A.P. was off exploring the hollers, Sara would be cooking, washing, sewing, and wrangling three kids.

A.P. cocked his head. "It's what we do, Sary."

She ducked her head. "Yes, it is."

A.P. hugged each of the children in turn, then kissed Sara's cheek.

Esley said, "Be good, you all."

I turned to Sue Dean. "See you again soon."

She nodded and held Joe close. I saw something in her eyes. It might have been anger, or it might have been hope.

Sara shot me a tired smile. "Take care of 'em, Nate. Not just the car."

"I'll try."

A.P. climbed behind the wheel, and Esley took the passenger side. I got in back. I smiled and thought, Just me and the hog.

We waved, then moved off down the road in search of a song.

CHAPTER 36

For me, it was mystery and adventure. For A.P., it was work.

Mr. Peer was always pushing for more songs, and A.P. didn't mind a bit. After recording the Carters in Bristol, he had brought them up to Camden, New Jersey, for more sessions. They recorded thirteen songs in two days, including "Keep on the Sunny Side," "John Hardy Was a Desperate Little Man," and "Wildwood Flower." The records came out a few months later, and still Peer wanted more. He had scheduled another Camden session for next February, so A.P. needed more songs, always more songs.

I learned all this in the back seat of the Chevrolet as we bumped along the road, headed south on Highway 91. I offered to help with the driving. I told A.P. and Esley about Mr. Lane's Packard and how I had driven it.

"Glad to hear that," said Esley. "We need all the drivers we can get."

After a while, I realized why. It turned out that A.P. wasn't the world's best driver. He would hum a song, and his mind would wander. The car would drift, and Esley would jerk the wheel back.

About that time, A.P. started humming and the car started drifting.

"Watch it!" said Esley, grabbing the wheel. "All right, that's it. Pull over."

"What for?" asked A.P.

"I'm driving."

A.P. snorted. "It's my car."

"It's my life," said Esley.

A.P. guided the car to a flat place by the road, where he and Esley swapped places. I had to admit I felt better. I think A.P. did too. Now he could hum to his heart's content.

We left Virginia, dipped into a corner of Tennessee, and came out the other side in North Carolina, traveling through little towns called Damascus and Laurel Bloomery. A short time later we entered Watauga County. Gazing through the car window, I tried to imagine Mama, Daddy, Sister, and me living there all those years ago. I pulled out the patched-up photo of Sister's grave and studied it. Maybe I'd be seeing it soon.

It turned out that A.P. and Esley weren't sure where Mandy Groves's friend lived, so we stopped for directions in Sugar Grove, a quiet town nestled in the mountains. They reminded me of my mountains—high, hazy, and, if the light was just right, a pretty shade of blue.

Then, directions in hand, we headed up some dirt roads

into the foothills. The car thumped and shimmied. We passed a few houses tucked back among the trees, and after a while I noticed A.P. gazing out the window, mumbling to himself.

"What are you doing?" Esley asked him.

"Counting."

"Counting what?"

"Mailboxes," said A.P.

"Well," said Esley, "when you got 'em counted, let us know."

"…eight, nine, ten. Lace. That's what they said."

"A.P., you're not making sense," said Esley.

"Stop!" said A.P.

Esley slammed on the brakes. I winced.

"Turn in here," said A.P.

"You think they have songs?" I asked him.

He stared at me. "No, I told you. Lace."

Esley glanced at me and rolled his eyes, like Arnie and I used to do. It made me smile.

A.P. pointed past the mailbox to a couple of faint tracks in the dirt that seemed to be a driveway. Esley sighed, spun the wheel, and bumped along the tracks to a stand of trees, where we found a cottage. Sure enough, there was a hand-lettered sign in the front yard: Lace. A.P. got out and headed for the door.

"What's he doing?" I asked.

Esley shrugged. "Doc—he marches to his own drum."

A.P. came back a few minutes later carrying a lace doily, like Mama used to put under flowerpots.

"You like lace?" Esley asked him.

"No, but Mandy told me her friend does. I figure it might help us get a song."

We pulled back onto the road, and it led into a narrow, winding canyon, a place I never would have noticed.

"You think someone lives in there?" I asked.

"Sure," said A.P. "Folks like the hollers, being off by themselves so they can follow the old ways."

At the end of the canyon, pressed up against the side of a mountain, was a shack that was painted bright purple. Esley parked in front of it, and we sat there.

"You going in?" I asked A.P.

He and Esley shared a look.

"We'll wait," said Esley. "First rule when you're hunting songs: let 'em come to you."

Ten minutes later, a woman stepped onto the porch. She was over six feet tall and as skinny as the rails I'd been riding.

In the car, Esley whistled softly. "She's bigger than Miss Mandy. Maybe there's a whole family of them—you know, Amazons, like those warriors in Greek mythology. I saw pictures of them in a book."

The woman wore coveralls and had long, gray hair that hung down to her waist, which was pretty far. She puffed on a pipe and stood there gazing at us.

A.P. rolled down his window and called, "Hattie Washburn?"

"Who's asking?" she said.

"A. P. Carter. You know, the Carter Family."

"Never heard of 'em."

"Mandy Groves said to look you up."

"Why?"

"Well, songs," said A.P.

"Go away," she said.

"Friendly ol' thing," whispered Esley.

"Shush!" hissed A.P.

He picked up the lace doily, opened the door, and edged out toward her, holding the doily in front of him like an offering.

She cocked her head and watched him approach. When he reached her, she took the doily and ran her fingers over it.

"Nice. Lula May Hodge?"

"Yes'm, we saw her just now," said A.P. "Beautiful work. It's yours if you'll give us a minute."

She puffed on her pipe. I caught a whiff, and I can tell you the tobacco didn't come out of a package. She admired the doily again, then stepped into the front yard, where an old wooden table was set up with four chairs. She folded herself into one of the chairs and nodded.

"All right," she said.

A.P. took a seat next to her. Esley motioned to me, and

we got out of the car. The minute Esley appeared, her eyes fastened onto him.

"Who's he?" she asked A.P.

"That's my guitar player, Lesley Riddle. The other one's my mechanic."

Esley got his crutch and guitar from the trunk, and the two of us joined them at the table.

"Nice house," said Esley. "Pretty color."

She puffed on the pipe, watching him all the while. "Painted it last month. I chose purple. That's Easter colors."

A.P. looked around at the autumn leaves. "Easter's in the spring."

She snorted. "Every day's Easter. Jesus rises like the sun. He picks radishes with me."

It was something Daddy might say. Somehow, though, coming out of her mouth, it didn't bother me.

A.P. cleared his throat. "Miz Washburn, I'll get to the point. I'm hunting songs. Mandy Groves gave me some good ones, and she thought you might do the same."

"Songs? What kind?"

"What do you have?"

She closed her eyes and started to sing. For such a big woman, she had a sweet, little voice, like Bernicia Flynn back in Daddy's church. Bernicia was eight years old.

It was a song about Jesus. Maybe it was her voice, but I imagined her as a young girl and wondered if she had smoked a pipe back then. She finished the song, then sang another and another. The woman was a walking hymnal.

I noticed that A.P. had pulled an envelope and a stubby pencil from his pocket and was scribbling as she sang, his hands shaking like they always did. Next to me, Esley fingered his guitar, picking out the tunes.

I like machines, and the Carter machine was running just fine. A.P. got the words. Esley got the notes. It was as sleek and efficient as Mr. Lane's Packard.

After twenty minutes or so, she said, "That's it."

"Now, Miz Washburn—"

Her eyes flashed. "That's it. Show's over."

Esley said, "We won't ask you to sing any more. But I have a question."

"What's that?" she asked, eyeing him suspiciously.

"There's a song—have you ever heard it?"

Esley nodded to me. A.P. looked on, puzzled. I took a deep breath and sang, while Esley played along.

Hattie Washburn scrunched up her eyes, like she was trying to spot something a long way off, on the horizon.

Finally she shook her head. "I don't think so."

Esley said, "Years ago? When you were young?"

"Nope. Sorry."

A.P. nodded politely. "Thank you for your kindness."

"What about my songs?" she asked him. "What'll you do with them?"

"Take 'em home. Roll 'em around. See what happens. If I like one, is it all right to use it? You know, on a record or concert?"

"Who did you say you are?"

"A. P. Carter of the Carter Family. We sing the old songs. People seem to like it."

"You think they'll like mine?"

"Hope so," said A.P.

"You wouldn't take out the Jesus, would you?"

"No'm. I'll leave him in."

She thought about it for a minute and said, "All right, then."

A.P. stuffed the envelope into his pocket, and Esley put his guitar in the case. As we headed for the car, A.P. turned back and said to her, "You sing good. Pretty as lace."

She blushed. People surprise you sometimes.

CHAPTER 37

We bumped down her driveway and got back on the road, with Esley behind the wheel again.

"Was she really that good?" I asked A.P.

"She was. Songs weren't. I've heard 'em a dozen times."

"You said you might record them."

"I always say that, just in case," he said. "I don't want to be accused of stealing."

"Do people ever say no?"

"Not so far."

Esley explained, "They're proud of the songs. They've handed 'em down for years. They want people to hear 'em."

"That song you did," A.P. told me. "I've heard it before."

My breath caught in my throat. "You have?"

"You sang it in Bristol when we were waiting in line."

I had to chuckle. A.P. was always picking up sounds, like Mr. Peer's recording machine.

"I like that first verse," he said. "Maybe we can ask around and find the other ones."

Esley steered the car out of the canyon and east on

Highway 421. The road wound through the hills. A warm breeze had started to blow. I knew because Esley liked to drive with the window down and his elbow hooked over the door.

My mind wandered back to Sue Dean, taking care of those children in Poor Valley. Neither she nor I had grown up in what you'd call a happy family, and now she was trying to reconstruct hers with some new parts. I wished her luck. I wished her more than that.

Soon the hills leveled off, and we passed some farms. I didn't think A.P. was paying attention, but suddenly he said, "Stop!"

Esley slammed on the brakes like before. I checked for cars behind us. Luckily, there weren't any.

"You know," I told A.P., "you should give him some warning."

But A.P. had other things on his mind. He got out, walked over, and stood with his hands on his hips, gazing down at something by the road.

Esley pulled off next to him, and we got out to see what it was. I figured A.P. had spotted a dead possum or raccoon, though I couldn't imagine why he would be interested.

When we got there, Esley said, "Not again."

We were staring at a rusty pile of metal.

"What is it?" I asked.

"Blades," said A.P. "Can't you see?"

I stepped closer and made out a jumble of what looked like

metal wheels, in various shapes and sizes, with teeth around the edges.

"For a sawmill," said A.P. "Let's take 'em, boys."

"A.P. started out working at a sawmill," Esley explained. "He still keeps an eye out for spare parts."

"Why?" I asked.

"Never can tell when you'll need one," said A.P. "Kinda like with songs."

I looked over at Esley, and he smiled.

A.P. told Esley, "Open the trunk." Then he said to me, "Come on, boy, lend a hand."

We loaded the rusty parts and headed off down the road. When we went over a bump, I could hear them in the back, clanging and clunking. A few minutes later, A.P. spoke up again.

"I'm hungry," he said.

If A.P. wanted something, he said so. I thought of my house, where you had to fix up your feelings before saying them—trim them, prep them, paint them with God. I liked A.P.'s way better.

We started looking for a place to eat, and a few miles on, we passed a little cottage by the road with a sign in front: Country Ham and Peanut Pie.

"Looks good," said Esley.

"Turn around," said A.P.

Esley did a U-turn, and we found a parking space in front

of the cottage. A couple of cars were next to us, along with a horse tied to a post. We got out, and to my surprise, A.P. and Esley walked by the front door and headed around the side.

"Where are we going?" I asked.

A.P. kept walking. There was a screen door in back, and A.P. knocked. A woman's face appeared behind the screen.

"Three hams, three peanut pies," said A.P.

"And three lemonades," said Esley.

The woman stared at Esley.

"Please, ma'am," he said.

She sighed, shook her head, and disappeared.

Esley said, "They won't serve me in front."

I started to ask why, then realized it was because Esley's skin was a different color from mine and A.P.'s.

A.P. said, "Esley goes to the back, we all go to the back."

The woman returned a few minutes later and handed us three brown paper sacks. A.P. pulled a crumpled-up bill from his pocket, flattened it out, and handed it to her.

"Keep the change," he said.

"Don't come back," said the woman.

It was still chilly outside, so we sat in the car and ate. The food was good, but the conversation at the door had left a bad taste in my mouth.

"Why couldn't we eat inside?" I asked, finishing my last bite of pie.

"Got our lunch, didn't we?" said A.P.

"It doesn't seem right."

A.P. studied me. "You ever see black people eat with white?"

"In the jungle," I said.

"The jungle!"

"It's a camp for hoboes."

"I'm talking about regular folks," said A.P.

I thought back to Bristol. "I guess not. But Daddy's church had black people."

"Your daddy's unusual," said A.P.

He wiped his mouth with a handkerchief. I collected the trash and put it in a can by the parking lot, then Esley got behind the wheel and we pulled back onto the highway. I thought of all the places A.P. and Esley had traveled together and wondered how often they had eaten in the car, maybe even slept there.

"I've spent time in Bristol," Esley told me. "Rough place for colored folks."

"Bristol? Really?"

He glanced back at me. "I think your Bristol is different from mine."

My Bristol was split in two. The hobo Bristol had a jungle. I wondered what Esley's Bristol was like. Maybe there were four or five Bristols, or six, or a dozen.

"Ever hear of the Klan?" asked Esley.

"I heard of them," I said. "Never saw them."

The Ku Klux Klan. KKK. People called it the Invisible Empire, and maybe it was. Like the wind blowing through the passenger-side window, you couldn't see it but you knew it was there. I'd heard people whisper the name, but when I asked my parents about it, they didn't want to talk.

"Klan says they're protecting white folks," said Esley, "but we're the ones need protecting."

I looked at A.P. to see what he thought, but he was humming softly to himself.

Esley said, "In this world, there's a line—black on one side, white on the other. If you step across, the Klan might come visit."

"And do what?" I asked.

"Well, the first time they might burn a cross on your lawn. Like a warning. The second time would be worse. You don't want a third time."

"Did they ever visit you?" I asked.

"Not so far. But they went to see my uncle Luther. Stubborn man—too stubborn."

"What happened?"

"They came in the night, wearing white sheets and hoods. Beat him up, threatened a lot worse. He wasn't as stubborn after that."

"You think that happens in Bristol?" I asked him, still puzzling over my hometown.

"Every month. Every week. But your mayor didn't like it.

He said, 'First hooded SOB who steps into my yard, I'll shoot him.' Brave man. Course, he lost the next election."

Esley shook his head. "I could have told him the Klan isn't the worst thing. The worst thing is jobs. The mills won't hire us. If you're black, you can be a janitor or a maid. These days you're lucky to find that."

I glanced over at A.P. to see what he thought, but he had barely heard. He was off in the hills someplace, pulled along by music.

"Where to?" asked Esley.

"South on Highway 194," said A.P., studying the map.

I looked over his shoulder. "To that little town? Valle Crucis?"

"You can wave as we drive by," he said. "We're going to the mountains."

PART VI

ROOM IN HEAVEN FOR ME

Beyond the sea where faiths of glorious beam
Where things abide that I have never seen
The soul's sweet home desperate never more
Will there be room for me on that bright shore

—A. P. Carter, "Room in Heaven for Me"

CHAPTER 38

The highway looped through the countryside, then up toward the hills, where there were endless creeks and hollers, all of which A.P. seemed to know. We would pass a holler, and he'd call out the name of a song he had heard there. Esley would hum it, and we'd pull in to see if they had any more. We slept in the car, and the folks we visited gave us enough food to get by. The food was important to Esley and me, but A.P. didn't much care. As far as I could tell, he ran on music.

We met pickers and singers, housewives and carpenters, farmers and weavers and hoboes, and every one of them had a song. For mountain people, it seemed that a song was as important as their name, and they were proud to share both. Afterward, I would share the verse of Mama's song, but no one seemed to recognize it.

Sometime, weeks later, we entered a town called Blowing Rock. A.P. knew a fiddler there who collected songs the way some people collect butterflies or stamps. Boone was next, where Esley met some people at the teachers college who let us stay with them. Leaving Boone, A.P. said it was time circle back toward home.

"I'd like to try one more place," Esley told him, glancing at me. "Ever been to Deep Gap?"

A.P. furrowed his brow. "Can't say as I have."

"It's Nate's home place. He said they have good music."

I had said no such thing but wasn't about to contradict him. My heart was suspended in my chest, split between Tennessee and North Carolina, forward and back, Daddy's tent and the picture in my wallet.

"I checked the map," said Esley. "It's ten miles up the road."

A.P. shrugged. "Let's go."

Deep Gap was just a few streets and buildings, what some people might call a "wide place in the road." Glancing around, I wondered what had brought Mama and Daddy there. I imagined them walking the streets, holding Sister's hand, pushing me in a baby carriage.

We parked in front of something called the Hello Café. A.P. and Esley set out searching for songs, while I went inside to do some searching of my own.

Behind the cash register stood a stout woman wearing an apron. I asked if she remembered Wilvur and Etta May Owens. She didn't, which surprised me in a town that small.

The woman asked, "When were they here?"

"They left in 1916. So maybe twelve years ago."

She turned to an older couple at a nearby table. "Wilvur and Etta May Owens—ever hear of 'em?"

The man looked at his companion, then shook his head. "Sorry."

"That's the mayor," the woman told me. "He knows everybody."

I asked her about the library, and she directed me to a small, cinder block building on the next street, where I was greeted by an elderly man with wire-rimmed glasses and a quick smile.

"Welcome! I love to see young people reading."

"Actually, I was looking for a city directory—1916? Maybe before?"

He led me to the reference section, which amounted to a couple of packing crates stacked sideways. I flipped through the books and hit pay dirt in a shabby 1915 directory. Wilvur and Etta May Owens were listed, along with an address. The strange thing was that there was no number, just a street: Callahan Road. The man pulled out a town map and showed me where it was.

"What kind of neighborhood is it?" I asked, excited.

He scratched his chin. "Not sure I'd call it a neighborhood. Go on over there—you'll see."

Deep Gap was tiny, so you could walk pretty much anyplace in town. But I didn't walk; I ran. I'd been digging, and my shovel had struck something hard. I was eager to pull it out and look at it.

I found Callahan Road. I stopped and stared. It wasn't much more than a dirt path with a street sign. There were no houses—in fact, no buildings at all. Empty fields stretched to the horizon.

In the distance was a barn with a farmhouse next to it. Determined to learn something, I made my way across a field and up a gravel driveway, passing chickens and a few cows on the way. Reaching the front door of the house, I knocked. The door opened, and a sandy-haired man peered out at me. He was gaunt, with a face like leather, and his bib overalls hung loose over a wrinkled shirt. He appeared to be middle-aged, but when I looked closer, I realized he was no older than thirty-five.

"Help you?" he grunted.

What could I say? *I'm searching for my past. I'm hunting my dreams. I'm a blank, and I want to be filled in.*

I told him, "My family lived here when I was little, in 1916. Maybe you've heard of my parents, Wilvur and Etta May Owens?"

The man shook his head. "Can't say as I have."

"The address said Callahan Road, but there are no houses."

"Never were," he said.

I waited for him to say more, but he didn't.

"Then where did they live?" I asked. My family seemed like a *they*, even though I had been part of it.

He gazed down the driveway to the road. "Back then, the place belonged to old Mr. Callahan. Got sick and had to sell it. He's gone now. Told me a family came and parked an old house trailer on that road. Called 'em squatters."

"Squatters?"

The man frowned. "He let 'em stay for a while if they helped with chores. Don't believe I'd have done that."

"Was their name Owens?" I asked.

"Didn't say."

I asked a few more questions, but that was all he knew. I wandered around the area, spotting a few people and asking them, then went back to town and did the same. No one had heard of them.

I was about to give up when I remembered the grave. It had been raining that night, and Daddy had gone to be with Sister. I hurried back inside the Hello Café, where the woman was cleaning off some tables.

"Is there a town cemetery?" I asked.

"By Brown's Chapel, up the old highway," she said, pointing.

The chapel was neatly kept and newly painted. Next to it, sure enough, was a small cemetery with rows of tombstones. I hurried up and down the rows, getting a glimpse of Deep Gap history. Some of the oldest graves went back to the late 1800s. Finally I found it, off on its own in a far corner. It was a simple stone marker. I took out the photo and held it up next to the marker.

Sweet Sister
1910–1916

She had only been six years old and always would be, a little thing for all the commotion she had caused, changing the course of three lives at the time and another one yet to come. At first it seemed odd that the marker showed no last name, but then I decided it was fitting. She was Sister, just Sister.

I looked up at the sky. Rain had fallen. Daddy had hugged the grave and, so they said, tried to climb in. What makes a person that sad and desperate?

"You seem to have found what you're looking for."

I turned around and saw a man wearing wrinkled pants with a work shirt and tie. He held out his hand, and I shook it.

"I'm Pastor Joe."

"Nate Owens."

He said, "I stumbled across that grave when I first came here three years ago. I was surprised there was no last name. I checked the records but couldn't find any information. I asked around. No one knew who she was." He chuckled. "I guess every town needs a mystery, and she's ours."

"She's mine," I said.

"Pardon me?"

"She was my sister. She died when I was two."

He at looked at me, amazed, then wanted to know all about her. Supposedly it was to fill in his records, but I knew that wasn't the reason. A little bit of our family mystery had spilled over onto him, and he wanted some answers.

Join the club, I thought.

I told him what little I knew. He wrote it down, thanked me, and headed back inside. Watching him go made me sad. Daddy was always preaching about Genesis, the beginning of things, when Satan tempted Eve and the world fell into sin. In my family, Deep Gap was our Genesis. Things had happened here—big things, important things, things that had changed our world. And the town had barely noticed.

CHAPTER 39

I sat on the steps of the Hello Café, and before long, A.P. and Esley came back.

"Any luck?" asked Esley, who knew what I'd been doing.

"They lived in a house trailer by a farm. That's all I know. It's all anyone knows. But I did see my sister's grave."

"You okay?" he asked.

I nodded. To be honest, though, I didn't know if I was okay or if I was anything.

"How did you do?" I asked him.

"Not much better."

"Heard a few hymns, none of them new," said A.P. "Esley sang your song once or twice. Nothing."

Esley brightened. "But we did find something. We met a young kid name of Watson, no more than five or six years old. Blind since he was a baby. His folks bought him a Sears Roebuck guitar, and he plays the fire out of that thing."

"I taught him one of our songs, 'When Roses Bloom in Dixieland,'" said A.P. "He picked it right up."

We climbed into the car and headed up Highway 421,

back toward Poor Valley.

"You said you heard hymns," I told A.P. "I didn't know you wanted those."

A.P. grunted. "We take hymns. We take all kind of things."

"Old ballads. Sheet music. Blues, definitely blues," said Esley. "Get 'em, throw 'em in the pot, and stir."

"We did a blues song for Mr. Peer in Memphis," A.P. said. "'Worried Man Blues.' He liked it. We should get some more of those."

Esley glanced over at him. A.P. nodded, and Esley nodded back.

"We're going home to Poor Valley," said Esley. "But on the way, we'll make a stop. I was born in North Carolina, but my grandparents raised me in Kingsport. Lotta blues there."

It turned out that Kingsport was where A.P. and Esley had met. I had grown up knowing Kingsport as one of Tennessee's tri-cities, along with Bristol and Johnson City. The three towns formed a triangle and were about twenty-five miles from each other. Kingsport had factories and mills, and workers went there from the hills of Tennessee, Virginia, and North Carolina. Esley told me there weren't many jobs these days, especially for Negroes, but the people went there anyway. He explained that when they weren't looking for jobs, some of the black workers would get together on a porch and play music.

"They heard blues music by Blind Lemon Jefferson, Barbecue Bob, folks like that," said Esley, excited at the memory. "Doc met them when he came looking for songs. John Henry Lyons had a good one called 'Motherless Children Sees a Hard Time.' When Doc showed up to hear it, I was sitting there with John Henry."

A.P. grunted. "Esley played along on a guitar. He sounded like Maybelle, only different."

"Nobody plays like Maybelle," said Esley.

"Didn't take the song," A.P. said. "Took the player."

Esley added, "I couldn't work in the factory because of my leg, so I had time to practice. When Doc heard me, he invited me home."

"Just like that?" I asked.

"Just like that."

"Nothin' else to do," said A.P.

Early in the afternoon we crossed the Tennessee border and entered Kingsport. The border didn't go through the middle of town, like it did in Bristol. It ran along the side, with the town right next to it.

We came into town on Route 1, which people in Kingsport called Lee Highway. As we did, the engine sputtered and died. Esley guided the car to the side of the road, and I opened the hood. He started it up, and I checked the engine. Finally I spotted the problem, a loose wire. I tightened it, and Esley grinned.

"Glad you came," he told me.

Esley turned off Lee Highway onto Sullivan Street. The road got wider, and the buildings got bigger. Pretty soon we came to a funny kind of intersection—round, with six roads jutting out of it. In between were churches, only churches, all of them with tall steeples.

Esley glanced over at me and laughed. "Your daddy's a preacher? He might call this heaven. Around here they call it Church Circle—Methodist, Baptist, Brethren, Presbyterian. Me, I call it White Church Circle."

"Where are the black churches?" I asked.

"I'll show you," said Esley.

We went through Church Circle and veered off to the right, into an area with train tracks and factories.

"There's one," he said, pointing to a broken-down building with a sign in front. On the sign, the words Pawn Shop had been crossed out and new words painted over it: Blessed Jesus AME Zion.

Thinking about the big, fancy buildings on Church Circle, it made me sad. If there was a God, I thought, he'd find the tents and pawn shops. According to the Bible, Jesus preferred them. I tried to picture Jesus in his sandals and dirty robe, wandering down the aisle of First Presbyterian Church. They'd hustle him out—or maybe just shoot him.

I watched the buildings go by. The farther we went, the smaller they got, until we turned onto a dead-end street that had just a few broken-down houses. Esley pulled up in front of one, a place that was neatly kept but badly in need of repair.

Esley elbowed A.P. "Hey, Doc, we're here."

"Play louder," murmured A.P.

"Wake up, Doc," said Esley. "End of the road."

A.P. stumbled from the car. Esley turned to me.

"Can you get the bags? You can leave the sawmill parts."

"Where are we?" I asked.

"The Kingsport Hotel," he said. "Better known as my cousin Caleb's house."

CHAPTER 40

Caleb turned out to be big and thick and tall, all the things Esley wasn't. There was a family resemblance though, in his eyes and easy manner.

"Back for more songs?" he asked, holding open the screen door.

"Got any?" said Esley.

"I don't, but George does. That's my neighbor, George McGhee. He got a job down at the factory, if you can believe it. He should be off pretty soon."

We trooped inside and followed A.P. down the hall to a bedroom. Obviously he had been there before. He flopped down on the bed. With A.P., it seemed that he was either exhausted or lit up like a red-hot coal. I told Esley I'd sleep in the car again, so he claimed a couch next to the bed and put his things there.

Caleb led us to the main part of the house, a combination kitchen, dining room, and living room. He cut up some cornbread, and he, Esley, and I visited for while at a rickety wooden table. Caleb and Esley caught up on family business, and Esley tried to explain how anybody, let alone three people, could make a living by collecting songs.

At four o'clock, a distant whistle sounded.

"Shift's over at the factory," said Caleb. "George is coming home."

Esley grabbed his guitar and woke A.P., then we headed down the street to the McGhee house. It was a modest place, painted and fixed up possibly when George got his job. There was a porch with steps, and something else too—a ramp to the front door.

As we approached, the door opened and a cart appeared. In it was a young Negro man who looked a little younger than me. Another young man came into view, pushing the cart. There was a strong family resemblance between them, with just a couple of differences—the one pushing was younger and thinner, and the one in the cart had a leg that was withered and folded under him.

"Hey, there, Brownie," called Caleb.

"Hey, Mr. Caleb," the one in the cart called back. "Hey, Esley."

Caleb said in a low voice, "That's George's son Walter. They call him Brownie. He had polio and can't walk. His little brother, Granville, pushes him everywhere in that wooden cart, so he's called Sticks."

As the brothers reached the bottom of the ramp, a car pulled up and a man got out. He was thin, with muscular arms and close-cropped hair. He wore a brown shirt that had a word stitched above the pocket: Maintenance.

"Hey there, George," said Esley.

The man saw me looking at his shirt and grinned. "Maintenance—funny word for a janitor, ain't it? Then again, maybe not. That's what I do. They holler at me, and I maintain."

Esley got up from the steps, hobbled over, and gave the man a hug, then turned to me. "Nate, this is George McGhee. Sings a mean blues. You got one for us, George?"

"Got twenty," said McGhee. "Which one you want?"

"The good one," said Esley.

McGhee went inside and came out wearing a different shirt—blue, with no words on it. He was carrying a tray that had a pitcher of sweet tea and some glasses. Sticks poured us some tea while his father disappeared again. When he came back, he was holding a guitar.

McGhee didn't sit. He just stood and sang like he was on a stage, and maybe he was. I noticed he was facing A.P., who had pulled out some paper and was scribbling on it. Next to A.P., Esley watched McGhee's fingers and tried to copy the chords.

McGhee sang us the good one, all right, then sang some more: "Stackolee," then something called "Frankie." I had never heard the songs before, but somehow, they sounded familiar. Maybe good songs are like that. Then he spun out some blues he made up on the spot, about women who cheated, men who loved them anyway, and factory jobs that paid the bills and not much else.

When he finished, we didn't clap. We didn't have to. The songs had grabbed us and squeezed. They were painful but also beautiful. After they ended, the sound floated in the air between us, shimmering like silver.

"Your daddy's good," I told Sticks.

"Yes, he is," the young man answered.

McGhee smiled. "Nothin' to it."

"Here's a song," said Esley, nodding to me. "We're trying to track it down."

So I sang. The words and music had lived inside my head, and now they were in the world, bobbing around, looking for a place to land.

McGhee cocked his head and smiled vaguely. "It's a pretty thing. Sorry though. Never heard it before."

"Hey," said Brownie, "you all want to stay for supper? Sticks and I can make biscuits and gravy."

A.P., hands trembling, stuffed the paper into his pocket and got to his feet.

"Thanks for asking," he warbled, "but we'd best be going. Gotta work on these songs—that is, with your permission."

"Honored," said McGhee. "Caleb told us about the Carter Family."

We walked back to Caleb's house, where he served us more cornbread and some black-eyed peas. Afterward, A.P. pulled out his paper and pencil to work on the songs.

"So," I said to Esley, "we leave in the morning?"

"Not quite yet. We got one more stop, right here in Kingsport."

"Another singer?" I asked.

Esley smiled. "You might say that. We're going to church."

CHAPTER 41

I was surprised to find that part of me had missed it—the preaching, the Bible reading, the feeling that, for a few minutes at least, I could just sit and think. I could put down my worries and stop asking questions. I could drink in the feelings all around me. Daddy called it worship, and I suppose it was, even for me.

We had gotten up early, thanked Caleb for his hospitality, and headed down the road to the church we'd seen earlier, Blessed Jesus AME Zion. The place had caught A.P.'s eye, and he wanted to go inside. I had planned to stay outside, remembering Daddy's tent and its stifling atmosphere, but then I saw how different this church was and finally agreed to go in.

It was in an abandoned store, with a display window toward the street and rows of folding chairs inside. The faces of the people were black, not white or mixed. Their brightly colored clothing shimmered in the cheap electric lights. The ladies' hats had broad brims, flowers, and enough fruit for a produce stand. The men's hats were small and elegant, some tipped at an angle over slicked-back hair.

The biggest difference wasn't anything you could see, but it filled the church to bursting. It was music.

Up front, wearing robes as blue as the sky, a choir sang and swayed. Some of them played tambourines. Off to one side, a robed man directed the choir with one hand and pounded an upright piano with the other. He wore thick glasses, but I had a feeling he could see everything he needed to without them.

Everybody sang—the choir, the ushers, the congregation. When the preacher spoke, I realized that he sang too, sometimes with notes and sometimes with words. The choir director answered on the piano, keeping a running conversation, and the people answered: "That's right." "Amen." "Preach it!"

Next to me, A.P. jotted notes on scraps of paper. Esley rocked with the music, and I could tell his recorder was running.

Sitting there, surrounded by music, I wondered once again why Daddy had shut it out of his church. If God wasn't in music, where was he? I'd traveled for weeks, running away but also searching for something. Here in this storefront with a crossed-out sign and a beat-up piano, I thought I might have glimpsed it. I didn't even know what it was. It was a little like science and a little like a song. It was a question with no answer. It was a feeling you got in your chest. It was big and deep and wide. It wasn't far away but was right next to you, or maybe inside. It seemed like a place you could stay forever. It felt like a home.

Esley glanced around the room, then looked over at me. "You like it?"

"Yes," I said.

I thought about my favorite singer—not the Carters, but Sue Dean. She wasn't famous, but she put her heart in the music. You could hear it swelling up in the notes and filling the empty spaces between. It was love that you could hear, that you could count on—or would like to. I wondered if she was at church that morning and decided she probably was, even if it was a church of her own. Here, there was music in the church. For Sue Dean, there was church in the music.

It was a good thing I enjoyed the service, because it lasted awhile—through the morning and past noon. Finally, about the time my stomach started growling, the choir sang its last *amen*.

The preacher greeted us at the door. "God bless."

A.P. mumbled an answer and walked off toward the car. Esley and I started to follow, but then I noticed an old man staring at me. I figured it was because I was white. I just smiled and nodded.

"You look like him," said the man.

"Like who?" I asked.

"Somebody I saw."

He gazed past me, looking at someplace far away. "Years ago, a white boy passed through town, singing and playing the banjo. Must have been sixteen, seventeen years old. He came to the church where I was going and played for a picnic. Can you imagine that? White boy playing at a black picnic?"

Esley, who was listening, grunted and chuckled.

"Thing is," said the man, "he was good. Not just white good or black good. Any color good. We had a wooden stage, and he climbed up on it. Once he got up there, he owned it. His face shone. His fingers flew across that banjo. And his voice? Lord, you should have heard it. Like a trumpet. God's own bugle. I never forgot that boy."

He looked back at me. "When I saw you in church, I thought he'd come back. I was sure of it. Then I thought, Hold on now, that was more than twenty years ago. Boy would be a man now. So, straighten me out. Who are you?"

"Nate Owens, sir. I'm just visiting."

"Owens, that was it!" said the man.

"Huh?"

"That was his name. Willie? William? Wilvur! Wilvur Owens. I wonder whatever happened to that boy."

CHAPTER 42

Oil and water don't mix. Black and white don't mix. Wilvur Owens and music don't mix. But they did.

If music is a sin, why had Daddy been singing? What had brought him to Kingsport, Tennessee? If he'd really played music, and if he'd been that good, why had he stopped?

I pictured Daddy preaching, stalking the stage, voice booming. The words turned to notes, and music poured out of him. All of a sudden, what had been unthinkable seemed not just possible but natural, maybe even inevitable.

But he hated music.

Dazed, I thanked the old man for the information, and he left. Esley turned to me.

"You want to tell me what just happened?"

I told him who Wilvur Owens was. I explained once again about the preacher and the tent and the sermons, and most of all the ironclad rule about music.

"Well now, that's strange," mused Esley.

We walked to the car, where A.P. was deep into his songs. Climbing in, we headed back to Poor Valley, with Esley behind the wheel again. The highway looped through the countryside, past Weber City and Hiltons. I wondered if my father had sung in those towns and why. No matter how strange or crazy he had seemed at times, his image had always been crystal clear in my mind. When the tent had come down, that picture had blurred. Now I wondered if I'd ever really seen him at all.

When we finally drove up to the house, Janette ran out to meet us. Little Joe, hair flying every which way, was right behind.

"Daddy!" cried Janette when A.P. got out of the car.

"Hello, darlin'," he said, accepting her hug.

Janette greeted Esley and smiled nervously at me. She was joined by Sue Dean, who picked up Joe. I wanted to touch her, but the best I could do was reach out and stroke Joe's cheek.

"Stop it!" he cried.

So much for reunions.

As we got our bags from the car, Gladys came through the door with Sara, who was wiping her hands on a dish towel.

"How'd it go?" Sara asked A.P.

He kissed her cheek awkwardly. "Got some songs for you. We'll work on them this week. Recording session coming up, you know."

Sara phoned Maybelle, and she came for supper with Eck and the children. I was happy to be included, like part of a family. I didn't say much at supper—just watched as Sue Dean ate, Sara and Maybelle chatted, Eck joked, and the children pestered Esley for stories. Sue Dean glanced over at me, but when I caught her eye, she looked away.

A.P. gulped down the last of his supper and moved to the sofa, where he arranged some scraps of paper beside him. Esley got his guitar and sat in a chair nearby. Picking out one of the papers, A.P. handed it to Esley.

"Got this song in Kingsport," he said.

Esley nodded. "I remember the tune."

He strummed a few chords, then picked out a melody. Sara came over and looked at the paper. While Esley picked, she sang, haltingly at first, then with more confidence.

> Everybody's got to walk this lonesome valley
> We've got to walk it by ourselves
> There's nobody here can walk it for us
> We've got to walk it by ourselves

Sara's sweet, pure voice floated across the room, brightening it like a candle.

> My father's got to walk this lonesome valley
> He's got to walk it by himself
> There's nobody here can walk it for him
> He's got to walk it by himself

Afterward, I found Sue Dean on the front porch, rocking in the swing and looking at the stars. I sat down beside her.

I said, "You ever feel lonesome? Like in the song?"

"Sometimes."

"I've been thinking about my father," I said.

I told her what I'd learned, about the young man who sang his heart out and looked like me.

"Your father?" she said. "How could that be?"

"I don't know. But I need to. I'm going back to Bristol."

"To stay?"

I shook my head. "To find out."

The crickets chirped. The swing creaked as we rocked.

"Would you come with me?" I asked.

She looked away. "I have work to do here."

"Just for a few days. You could ask."

"Why would I do that?"

We swung for a little while longer. Then she got up and went inside. The swing seemed empty. I felt lonely again.

A few minutes later, she came back. "I talked to Sara. It's okay."

"You'll come?"

"Don't get any ideas," she said.

CHAPTER 43

The next morning at breakfast, I told A.P. that I'd like a few days off.

"I need to take care of some things," I said.

A.P., buttering a biscuit, barely looked up. "Sary told me. Esley and I are staying here, fixing up songs, so I guess we won't need a mechanic for a little while."

"Or a car," volunteered Esley. "What do you say, Doc? Could he take yours?"

A.P. shrugged. "Don't see why not."

I'd been planning to ride the rails again, but having Sue Dean on the trip had complicated things. Now, suddenly, it would be simple.

We packed a few things and headed out later that morning. I felt good driving the car by myself, and even better having Sue Dean along. The car was like our own little world.

"What are you thinking?" she asked as we headed down the road.

"It's sort of like the cabin," I said. "Just you and me."

She didn't say anything. She just looked out the window.

For me, the cabin was the two of us, heads together, listening to the crystal set. For her, it might be something different—a note, a goodbye never spoken.

We drove west along the base of the mountains, then turned south. After a while we joined up with Highway 11, which took us through Abingdon and on into Bristol, from the Virginia side.

We arrived late that afternoon. The first thing we saw was the Bristol sign, bordered by electric lights. A good place to live, it said. Maybe it was for some. We drove down State Street, along the border that divided the town. It was just a line on a map, but it was real. I felt it.

I guided the car into the neighborhood where we had lived, past the cemetery and toward the vacant lot where the big yellow tent had stood. Some boys were using the lot to play baseball, yelling and kicking up dust. I pulled over, and we watched them for a minute. So much of my early life had taken place on that lot, but I didn't claim to understand it. The boys didn't care. They laughed and hit and ran the bases, trying to reach home.

Next to the vacant lot was the little white house where I'd grown up. The paint was fading, and the place seemed smaller. I parked in front. Sue Dean and I got out, went up the front walk, and knocked on the door. It swung open, and a boy stood there.

"Arnie?" I said.

I'd been gone just a few months, but he had changed. He was eleven years old, though looking at him you'd think he was older. His face was lined. His shoulders were hunched, and his hands were curled like claws. His energy and spirit, which Mama had wanted to bottle, were nowhere in sight.

He smiled, but it was more like a grimace. "Nate!" Stepping forward, he put his arms around me. They felt stiff and awkward.

Pulling away, I said, "You remember Sue Dean, don't you?"

He eyed her warily. "I thought you left."

"I did," she said.

I asked Arnie, "Are you...okay?"

He glanced down at his hands and shrugged. "I look like an old crow."

"What happened?"

"Beelzebub," he said. "Like Daddy said, he won't let you go."

"The snake?"

Arnie nodded. "After you left, I started getting pains in my hands and arms. My shoulders drew up. My body ached. Doctor said it was the snake. Rattler bites can hurt for a long time."

I remembered the day when Arnie had walked down the aisle with Beelzebub coiled around his neck. Once again I wondered what would drive anyone to do that. Whatever it was, Daddy had it and so did Arnie. Maybe it changed over time, the way Arnie's body was changing—twisting up, curling in on itself.

He held the door open, and we stepped inside. Sniffing the air, I caught a whiff of floor wax and cornbread, along with the candles Mama lit before bedtime. It was the smell of my house, my family, my life from before. At the time, I'd barely noticed it, at least not any more than I'd noticed Daddy's weird, shouted prayers or the way Arnie whimpered in the night.

Arnie led us into the kitchen, where Mama stood at the stove with her back to us.

"Who was it?" she called to Arnie.

"Hello, Mama," I said.

Turning around, she launched herself at me, grabbing and holding on tight. When she pulled away and looked me over, her cheeks were wet.

"I wish I could have done that before you left," she said. "You didn't give me the chance."

"If I did, I never would have gone. I needed to leave."

"Where did you go?"

"It's a long story." I spotted potatoes and string beans on the stove. "Could I tell you over supper?"

Mama asked me to set the table as if I'd never left. Sue Dean helped. Halfway through, Daddy came in. He grabbed me too. Our family had its share of problems, but hugging had never been one of them. Daddy hugged me so tight I didn't know if he had missed me or wanted to kill me.

I was all set to dive in to the mashed potatoes when Daddy

took hold of my hand and I remembered. Before eating, we always clasped hands around the table and prayed—or rather, Daddy prayed.

This one was a doozy. It was your basic Prodigal Son theme, with some Children of Israel mixed in. It seemed that I had run off, staggered through the desert, spent time in a pigsty, then been welcomed home to eat the fatted calf, or in this case, cornbread and black-eyed peas. Daddy might not have a big audience anymore, but his pipeline to God was still open.

A week later, when the prayer ended, I took a gulp of sweet tea and told them what really had happened—no desert, no pigs, no food. Trains and the people who rode them. I described Bill and his band of angels. I told them about the jungle, leaving out the girl who stole my pack. I took them on a trip to Gate City and into the home of the woman named Dolly.

"What happened there?" asked Arnie.

I took a deep breath. I had come a long way, and I wasn't about to stop.

"Music," I said.

Daddy glanced up sharply. Arnie and Mama looked away.

"We don't talk about that here," said Daddy.

"Don't you want to know what happened?" I asked.

Mama put her hand on his. "Let him talk, Wilvur."

He lowered his head, and she nodded to me. I told about

the Carter Family—how Sue Dean and I had met them in Bristol, how I'd heard their records at Dolly's house, and how the records had drawn me to Poor Valley, where I'd found Sue Dean.

"We work for the Carters," I told them proudly. "Sue Dean watches their children. I keep their car running. I'm a mechanic."

Daddy looked up again. "That's quite a story."

"You haven't heard the best part."

He cocked his head, and I almost felt sorry for him.

"I went to a church in Kingsport," I told him. "A man said he had heard you."

"That's good," said Daddy.

"You weren't preaching. He said you sang and played the banjo."

CHAPTER 44

For a second I thought he might cry. Then his face hardened
and he looked away.

I leaned forward. I felt electric, like the battery in A.P.'s
Chevrolet. "The man said you were good. He called you
God's trumpet."

"Blasphemy," Daddy growled.

"Is it true?" asked Arnie. "What Nate heard? Mama, is
it true?"

Mama was gazing at Daddy. She didn't speak or move.
She was a tuning fork, picking up Daddy's moods and vibrat-
ing with them. Thinking back, it had always been like that.

I told him, "The man thought I was you. He said we
looked just alike."

Daddy just sat there.

"I love music," I said. "So did you. What happened?"

Something in his eyes told me he had gone back. He was
there, in a time before I was born, remembering what it had
been like. I thought I might see happiness or pride. What I
saw was pain.

Next to me, Sue Dean shifted in her chair. I had told her about my family, and now she was seeing it close up.

"Music is beautiful," I said.

He muttered, "You're stubborn. You always were."

"It's not a sin," I told him.

He turned his gaze on me. His face was pale, drained of life. The look he gave me was so cold that it burned.

"You're not welcome here."

"Wilvur!" said Mama.

She took Daddy's hand, and he pulled away.

"You can finish your supper," he told me. "You can spend the night. But tomorrow morning, you need to go."

Daddy got up, placed his napkin on the table, and walked out of the room.

***

I had trouble sleeping. I kept thinking about Daddy on that stage, singing. Daddy in the tent, preaching. Daddy gripping my head, praying. Daddy kissing me good night.

When I was little, before the tent or the snake, sometimes I'd have nightmares. If they were especially bad, I would tip-toe from my room, out the back door, and across the backyard to the shed. I'd tinker in the moonlight, fiddling with Daddy's tools. It made me feel better.

I got up, pulled on a bathrobe, and went down the hall past Arnie's room, past the room where Sue Dean was sleeping. I pushed open the back door.

The night was warm. The stars glittered. They had traveled with me along the rails and had followed me home. They seemed like friends, but they were as cold and stark as the look Daddy had given me.

I was halfway to the shed when I heard a voice. It was familiar but different, like a favorite portrait that's been gripped in a fist, then used for a different purpose—to swat a child or kill a spider.

The voice was angry. It was rough and tortured. It had power. It wasn't a trumpet. It was more like a drum or a thunder clap.

Daddy was singing.

> Oh Death,
> I prayed you wouldn't call so soon.
>
> I glimpse a face in the dark'ning sky,
> A twisted grin, an eyeless eye,
> A bony hand of purest white,
> Who goes there in the black of night?
>
> Do you not know? Well, listen then.
> 'Tis I who conquer sons of men,
> And no one from my curse is free.
> My name is Death, and time serves me.

I hone the blade. I plunge the knife.
I seize the thing you call your life.
I fire the gun. My aim is true.
Prepare yourself. I come for you.

Oh Death,
I prayed you wouldn't call so soon.

I stood in the doorway of the shed, watching. I thought of the people in the graveyard across the street. They'd struggled, and death had won. Daddy was still fighting, but barely.

He finished, lowered his head, and stood there for a long time. He was crying.

I didn't know him. Until I left home, I'd been with him nearly every day of my life, but the man standing in the shed was a stranger. I thought of all that I'd missed because of it. There's a well deep inside of us. The water churns. Sometimes it's clear and cold. Other times it's muddy. It has a taste that only we know. I think Daddy's well was deeper than most. I wondered what was at the bottom.

I must have moved, because he looked up and saw me.

"Get out," he said.

"No."

"You don't belong here."

"I'm your son. A man thought I was you."

"I tried to teach you," he said. "I never knew if I was getting through."

"The good things did."

His face filled with pain. "Music?"

"It's important, Daddy. It's beautiful. I believe in it."

"Believe in God," he said.

"Maybe it is God."

He flinched. "Don't say that."

"It's as close to God as we get. You used to think so, didn't you?"

"I was young."

"I heard you just now," I said. "You still believe it."

He sighed. "Twelve years. That's how long it's been."

"Since you sang?"

"Since everything."

There was a worktable off to one side of the room. Daddy's toolbox was on top of it. Beside that was Beelzebub's cage, empty now. Next to the table were a couple of stools. Daddy shuffled over and sat down on one. I took a seat next to him.

He stared. I wondered what he saw.

Finally, he said, "She was so pretty."

"Sister?" I asked.

It was the subject he always returned to. I guess she was always there, just below the surface.

He nodded. "I used to hold her and rock her to sleep."

"I barely remember her."

"Her hair was curly. Her eyes were bright. She had a dimple by the corner of her mouth. But she got sick."

"Typhoid fever," I said.

"That's right."

He took a deep, ragged breath. I could tell it hurt, like he was breathing fire.

"I was gone," he said.

"What do you mean?"

He spit out the words. "I was out of town. I was playing music."

The world stopped. A door opened just a crack. I didn't dare touch it for fear it would swing shut.

He said, "I had a band—guitar, fiddle, mandolin, bass. I played the banjo and sang. We lived in North Carolina but traveled all over. Did picnics, festivals, weddings. White, black, you name it."

"Did you play at Kingsport?"

"Many times. By the time Sister came along, I'd been singing for years. Started when I was your age, like the man said."

He looked away, and I could tell he was back there. "I married your mama after high school. Kept singing. Sister came along. Kept singing. Sister got sick—fever, pain, a bad cough. Kept singing.

"The band was booked at a county fair in Raleigh that weekend. I could have stayed home with Sister, but I didn't. I wanted to play music. I loved it. I loved it too much.

"We played so well at the fair. I sang better than ever. When I got home, Sister was dead. They said before she passed, she was asking for me. But I wasn't there. I left her because of music. And I knew right then, the only thing that could keep me from my daughter was the devil. Satan did it. It was his music. So I put down my banjo and never played it again. I dedicated my voice to God—not to sing, but to preach."

"Why didn't you tell me this?" I asked.

"You didn't need to know."

"Yes, I did." Listening to him sing had made me ache. "You shouldn't have kept it from us."

"I was afraid to tell you, because I thought you might take up music. I guess I was right."

I looked back at where he had stood a few moments before, calling out to death, ripping the scab off an old wound.

I asked, "What was that you were singing?"

"They say it's a folk song."

"It scared me."

"I think it rose up straight out of the earth. Like a corpse. Like bones when they've been picked clean."

I shivered. I didn't much remember Sister, but it hurt to think of her lying in the ground.

I took the photo from my wallet and set it on the bench. Sister was with us, or at least her grave was.

"I went there," I said. "To Deep Gap. To the cemetery. I have the memory. I don't need the picture anymore."

Daddy picked up the photo and ran his fingers across it.

"She's in heaven now," he said.

"You believe that?"

"With all my heart."

He had to believe. Maybe I did too. But my idea of heaven was different from his.

"What about me?" I asked.

"Huh?"

"You did all this for Sister. Gave up music. Started the church. What about me?"

He stared at me like I was speaking another language.

"Sister's gone," I said. "But she's not the only one."

He shook his head. "What do you mean?"

"I left too. I'm leaving again."

Feelings rolled around inside of me. I tried to put them into words. "You spent all those years thinking about Sister. Feeling guilty. Taking the blame. But you know what? She's not coming back. I'm sorry to say it, but it's true."

He hunched over, hugging himself, like he was in pain.

"There was nothing you could do for her," I said. "But I'm still here. So is Arnie. Stop thinking about Sister and worry about us."

Daddy looked up, startled. "Worry?"

"I was miserable. So I left. You ran me out of town. And Arnie? You drove him to that snake. He's sick. He needs you."

Daddy gaped at me. For all the times he had talked to God,

he had never heard that. He was shocked to hear it, and I guess I was too. A minute before, I had been angry. Now I just felt sad.

"Daddy, I know it's hard. She was your angel. She was your favorite."

"That's not true."

"You know it is. You showed it every day."

"I love all my children," he said.

"Then do something."

"She was so precious."

"All of us are. Isn't that what Jesus said?"

The night settled in around us. Crickets chirped. In science class, Mr. Wafford had told us that crickets chirp by rubbing their wings together. If they could play music, surely we could too.

"So," I said, "now what do we do?"

"Pray. Preach."

"Sing," I said.

CHAPTER 45

Daddy didn't come to breakfast the next morning. I had wanted to see him, if only to say goodbye.

I knew that in spite of what I'd told him—maybe because of what I'd told him—I needed to leave. It was just too painful.

We got up at sunrise. Mama cooked up some eggs and sausage. I had coffee, which I'd started drinking to keep me awake on the road. No one said much. I think Mama was sad. Arnie had questions but didn't know how to ask them or whether he was allowed. I don't know what Sue Dean thought. She ate quietly.

As for me, the room seemed dark and full. Something was in there with us. It hung over the table like a cloud, like a spirit that settles in and won't go away. I guess it had been there all along, crowding us, shaping us, keeping us down. It pressed against my chest until finally I had to say something.

"I couldn't sleep last night."

"Did you open a window?" asked Mama.

"I got up and went outside. Daddy was in the shed."

Arnie looked up at me. "The shed?"

To him that had one meaning—Beelzebub. I couldn't tell if he was excited or scared.

"Daddy was singing," I said.

They stared at me, all but Sue Dean. For her, singing was as natural and inevitable as breathing.

"That's good, isn't it?" she said.

"It's creepy," said Arnie.

I told them how he had sung about death. Then, because I was sick of the feeling that filled the room and wanted to puncture it and drain it dry, I told them what had happened all those years ago. It was Daddy's story, but it was ours too. Mama already knew it, of course. For Arnie, it was different. The thought of Daddy roaming the countryside, singing, was like being told that Jesus played ping-pong.

Mama said, "I tried to tell him it wasn't his fault. Sister took a turn for the worse and suddenly was gone. But he had wanted to be there. He had wanted to hold her hand. He blamed himself and music. Never forgave either one."

"Music's a sin, isn't it?" asked Arnie.

"Your daddy thinks so," said Mama.

"Then why was he singing last night? What does it mean?"

"I'm not sure, dear."

Part of me wanted to stay until I could work it all out and explain it to Arnie. But another part was eager to get back on the road, explore the hollers with A.P. and Esley, then return home to Sue Dean and the family I had found.

I turned to Sue Dean. "Ready to go?"

"I think so." She told Mama, "Thank you for having me."

Mama looked from Sue Dean to me and back at her again. "You're a nice girl. You take care."

Arnie said, "Do you have to go?"

"Yes," I told him. "But I'll come back."

As we started to get up, the kitchen door swung open. Daddy stood there, carrying a battered instrument case. He crossed the room and pushed aside the breakfast dishes. Setting the case on the table, he opened it. Inside, covered with dust, was a banjo.

Suddenly I was back in Daddy's tent. At the end of the service, he would ask for people to have their things blessed by setting them on the altar, the one that Arnie had made out of a soapbox. People would come forward and set things down—a ring, a family Bible, a pair of glasses. One woman stood there empty-handed, then reached into her mouth and set her dentures on the altar. We would pray over the objects, asking the Lord to bless them and consecrate them to his use.

I looked down at the banjo and wondered if Daddy would pray over it. He didn't say a word.

Arnie reached out and plucked a string.

"That's not how you do it," said Daddy.

He picked up the banjo. At first he handled it like something delicate, crystal maybe, or Mama's china. Using a napkin, he wiped off the dust ever so gently, then plucked the strings and adjusted the tuning pegs. He strummed a chord. It sounded good. He relaxed, and suddenly the banjo seemed as natural in his hands as one of the tools in his shed.

Daddy looked at me, then closed his eyes. Maybe he was conjuring up the young man who sang at Kingsport. He might be imagining a world, one that somehow had room for both God and music. It was a strain, I could tell. His brow furrowed, and his lips were pursed to one side. He picked out a melody and started to play. He shook his head and sang, haltingly at first, then with more confidence.

> Lord of the mountain
> Father on high
> Bend down and bless me
> Please won't you try

It was Mama's song. It had lived in our house all those years, like one of the candles she kept by her bed. The wind blows, and you cup your hands around it. It flickers and nearly dies. Then the wind lets up, and the flame leaps. You watch, amazed that what seemed to be snuffed out had been there all along.

> Give me a prayer
> Give me a plan
> Give me an answer
> I know you can

When he paused, I said, "That song—where did it come from?"

"I wrote it," he said. "Sister was sick, and I wanted to make her feel better. Mama and I used to sing it when we sat up with her. I performed it once or twice with my band, but it didn't feel right."

I imagined a room late at night in Deep Gap, North Carolina. A man and woman sat in the darkness with their little girl. The girl moaned. The mother held her hand. The father wiped her forehead tenderly, humming a tune. In the next room, a toddler slept, not knowing that what was taking place would shape his life.

"We lived in a house trailer," I said.

"How did you know?" asked Daddy.

"I went there, like I told you. I wanted to find out what happened. I sang the song. I walked the road. I found the grave. I asked if people remembered you. No one did."

Mama smiled sadly. "We had that trailer, so we moved a lot. We were only in Deep Gap for one year, when Sister was sick. We didn't go out much. Afterward, we sold the trailer and came to Bristol."

"Why didn't you tell me all this?" I asked.

Mama looked at Daddy. "We were trying to forget."

I said, "The song is beautiful. I bet Sister liked it."

"I sang it for her when Daddy was gone," said Mama. "I sang it as she died. It was the last thing she heard."

Tears rolled down Daddy's cheeks. Mama told him, "Your song was with her. You sang her to heaven."

He strummed the banjo and sang again.

> I'm feeling weary
> Tired to the bone
> Show me the path, Lord
> I'm going home

His voice was different from the night before. It was rough. It creaked, like something that hadn't been used in a long time. But there was a sweetness to it. Music floated across the room, brightening it like the sun.

> Over the hilltop
> Into the blue
> Home to the mountain
> Resting in you

When he finished, Sue Dean smiled. "Sing it again."

"I can't," he told her.

"I'll help you," she said.

Gingerly, he picked the banjo strings. The tune formed. He raised his voice. Sue Dean moved over next to him, put her hand on his shoulder, and joined in.

As they harmonized, my mind drifted back. I remembered

the first time I had heard the Carters sing, in the building that used to be a hat company. I'd been looking for answers and had thought I could find them behind the curtain, in the recording machines. I hadn't known it, but the answers were in front of the curtain, out in the room and in the world. Science asks questions and helps to answer them, but maybe some questions are in the heart and can only be answered there.

I sipped my coffee and listened. As I did, the earth shifted. Pieces fell into place. Two became one—tent and phonograph, science and snakes, dreams and music.

Gazing out the window, I saw the sun rise over the ridge. A mockingbird chattered. The breeze blew. Holston Mountain glowed.

AUTHOR'S NOTE

Years ago, when I moved to Nashville, I didn't care for country music. But as time passed, the music seeped into me, and I came to appreciate its rich history, culture, and storytelling tradition. In particular, I became fascinated with the people who brought their songs with them from the old country, settled in the Appalachian Mountains, and molded the music to fit a new world and a tough, demanding life.

I also became fascinated with the role of religion in their lives and the way music and church so often went together. Could the two ever be separated? Was it even possible?

Out of these musings came the character of Nate Owens, who loves music and deeply resents church, or at least the version of church preached passionately and interminably by his evangelist father. Through Nate, I began to explore my own feelings about music, faith, and how they intersect and overlap in our lives.

Nate, Sue Dean, Gray, their families, and a few minor characters in this story are fictional, but most of the other people and many of the things they do are based on fact. This includes the Carter Family, Lesley Riddle, Ralph Peer, and the events that became known as the Bristol Sessions, the so-called "big bang" of country music. In truth, of course, it wasn't an explosion; it was more like a river, deep and wide, that flowed from a thousand sources. But after those two weeks in Bristol, a musical tradition that had been pushed to the margins could never again be ignored.

I loved getting to know these people, real and imagined, and traveling with them on the road and over the rails. I'm grateful to those who showed me the way, including the authors who first got me excited about the people and their story: Mark Zwonitzer and Charles Hirshberg in their book *Will You Miss Me When I'm Gone?: The Carter Family & Their Legacy in American Music*; Barry Mazor in *Ralph Peer and the Making of Popular Roots Music*; and Ted Olson and the late, great dean of country music historians, Charles K. Wolfe, in *The Bristol Sessions: Writings about the Big Bang of Country Music*. I learned about teenage hoboes of the 1920s and '30s from Lexy Lovell and Michael Uys's fine documentary film *Riding the Rails*. Thanks to the helpful folks at the Bristol Public Library, Nashville Public Library, Vanderbilt University Library, Tennessee State Archives, Railroad Museum of Virginia, and Birthplace of Country Music Museum.

I've reshaped, redirected, and revised this story more times than I care to count, guided by my wonderful editors Jon Westmark and Kristin Zelazko at Albert Whitman & Company and my agent Alec Shane at Writers House. And always, standing at my shoulder to root me on, are my late parents, my family and friends, and my two shining stars, Yvonne and Maggie.

Helen Burrus

RONALD KIDD is the author of fourteen novels for young readers, including the highly acclaimed *Night on Fire*. His novels of history, adventure, comedy, and mystery have received the Children's Choice Award, an Edgar Award nomination, and honors from the American Library Association, the International Reading Association, and the New York Public Library. He is a two-time O'Neill playwright and music fan who lives in Nashville. You can learn more at www.ronaldkidd.com.

100 Years of

Albert Whitman & Company

1919–2019

Albert Whitman & Company encompasses all ages and reading levels, including board books, picture books, early readers, chapter books, middle grade, and YA

Present

2017 — *The Boxcar Children* celebrates its 75th anniversary and the second Boxcar Children movie, *Surprise Island*, is scheduled for 2018

2014 — The first Boxcar Children movie is released

2008 — John Quattrocchi and employee Pat McPartland buy Albert Whitman & Company, continuing the tradition of keeping it independently owned and operated

1989 — *Losing Uncle Tim*, a book about the AIDS crisis, wins the first-ever Lambda Literary Award in the Children's/YA category

1970 — The first Albert Whitman issues book, *How Do I Feel?* by Norma Simon, is published

1956 — Three states boycott the company after it publishes *Fun for Chris*, a book about integration

1942 — *The Boxcar Children* is published

1938 — *Pecos Bill: The Greatest Cowboy of All Time* wins a Newbery Honor Award

1919 — Albert Whitman & Company is started

Early 1900s — Albert Whitman begins his career in publishing

Celebrate with us in 2019!
Find out more at www.albertwhitman.com.